MW00625487

CERNUNNOS BOOKS

The Dancer, Her Lover and the Yogi

BHAGWATI CHARAN VERMA

Bhagwati Charan Verma (1903-1981) made seminal contributions to Hindi literature and film over a long career. He wrote *Chitralekha* (the original work that this book is a translation of—*Chitralekha* literally means "one who is as pretty as a picture") in 1934. He had some published works to his credit at the time, but *Chitralekha* gave him unparalleled acclaim. He became a full-time writer after this success. Bhagwati Charan Verma worked for Bombay Talkies, a movie studio founded in 1934, and wrote scripts for several films including *Kismet* (Fate, 1943), *Hamaari Baat* (Our Conversation, 1943), *Jwaar Bhaataa* (The Tides, 1944) and *Pratima* (The Image, 1945). Two Hindi films were based on *Chitralekha*. In 1950, he returned to Lucknow and devoted himself to literature. He won the Sahitya Akademi Award for his epic five-part novel *Bhoole Bisre Chitra* (Forgotten Pictures) in 1961. He produced more than fifty works of prose, fiction and autobiography. He won many awards and honours, and was nominated to be a member of the Rajya Sabha, the upper house of the Indian parliament.

ARCHANA VERMA

Dr. Archana Verma (born 1946) obtained an MA with six gold medals from Allahabad University and she holds MLitt. and Ph.D. degrees from Delhi University. She taught at the Department of Hindi, Miranda House, Delhi University from 1966 to 2011. She co-edited the Hindi literary magazine Hans with Rajendra Yadav from 1986 to 2008. Subsequently, she has been associated with the Hindi literary magazine *Kathadesh*, in which she has regularly authored an acclaimed column, *Prasangvash* (By the Way) for five years. Dr Verma is the author of a young adult novel and two collections each of short stories, poems and literary criticism. She has edited the collected works of Rajendra Yadav (in fifteen volumes) and co-edited and co-directed a series of translations titled *Hashiye Ulanghti Aurat* (Women Crossing Boundaries).

PRATIBHA VINOD KUMAR

Pratibha Vinod Kumar published her first work, a translation of the Hindi epic *Kamayani*, in 2013, at the age of 72. This is her second translation. She taught English at St. Michael's School, Durgapur, India from 1966 to 1985, and Rotary Public School, Gurgaon, India from 1985 to 1991. A.K. Kulshreshth is her son's pen-name.

BHAGWATI CHARAN VERMA

THE DANCER, HER LOVER AND THE YOGI

CHITRALEKHA

With an afterword by Archana Verma
Translated by Pratibha Vinod Kumar and A.K. Kulshreshth

Cernunnos
BOOKS

This translation © 2015 by Cernunnos Books Pte. Ltd., Singapore

All rights reserved. No part of this book may be reproduced in any form without written permission from the publisher.

Originally published in Hindi as *Chitralekha* in 1934. Translated rights granted by Shri Vijay Pratap Singh Verma on behalf of the copyright owners.

Hindi advisors: Archana Verma and Balwant Kaur

Cover design by Zoya Chaudhary

Literary editors: Desiree Ward, Nolwen Henaff

Interior design: 52 Novels

ISBN: 9789810994426

PROLOGUE

nd sin?" Shwetank asked.

Guru Ratnambar, the Great Mentor, started like a man disturbed in a deep sleep. He looked at Shwetank gravely. "Sin? It is a very difficult question to answer, young man, but it is natural to ask. So, what is sin?" He looked towards Patliputra, whose proud skyscrapers were still visible in the dim crimson evening glow. "Well, I have tried many a time to define sin, but I have never succeeded. What is sin? Where does it exist? This is a great problem. To this day, I have not been able to solve it. When I failed to unravel this secret in spite of my incessant efforts and my ocean of experience, how can I explain it to you?"

After a pause, Ratnambar spoke again, "But Shwetank, if you want to find its true nature, you will have to seek it in the real world. If you are ready for it, it is possible you may find the meaning of sin."

Shwetank bowed to Ratnambar. "I am ready."

Ratnambar looked at Vishaldeva and said, "Perhaps you too would like to try to understand the nature of sin?"

Vishaldeva bowed. "The Great Mentor is right."

Ratnambar's face lit up with happiness. "It is necessary that I make you aware of the circumstances before I have you gain experience by going out into the world and wandering in it. I know two prominent gentlemen of the city. To fulfil your task you will surely need their help. One of them, Kumaragiri, is a yogi and the other, Beejgupta, is a man of the world. Your lives will have to follow the flow of theirs."

"We agree," both disciples said in unison.

"Vishaldeva, you are a *brahman*. You like meditation and devotion, so it will suit you to be Kumaragiri's disciple. And Shwetank, you are a *kshatriya*, a man of the world, so you will serve Beejgupta.

The disciples again said, "We agree to do so."

"Your paths have been chalked out," Ratnambar said. "Now I will be out of the picture. Do not worry for me. Experience is as important in life as worship. You both will gain experience, and I shall be the ascetic. One year from this day, you both must meet me here. And then we will again proceed on our destined paths." Shwetank marvelled at the simplicity with which the Guru reached such a major decision.

"But do remember," Ratnambar continued, "I am sending you out into the world to learn from experience what you cannot learn from study. You must take care that you do not drift in the currents of the world. You will find yourselves floating among the waves of your worldly lives, and you must be careful not to drown."

Shwetank and Vishaldeva looked at each other.

Ratnambar broke the silence. "Let me brief you on the circumstances that you will find yourselves in. Kumaragiri is a yogi; he claims to have conquered all the desires of the world. He is dispassionate and detached. He holds that he has realised true bliss. He has vigour and charisma, physical and mental strength. People say that he has mastered his emotions. He is young, but youth and celibacy have given him a divine aura. To him the world is a means to achieve his goal of heaven. This Kumaragiri will be your guru, Vishaldeva."

Ratnambar paused for a while. He took a deep breath and seemed to revel in the fresh morning air tinged with the scent of mud and hay. He turned to Shwetank. "And Shwetank," he said, "Beejgupta revels in the senses. His heart is filled with the ardour of youth, and his eyes have the red tinge of intoxication. Sensual pleasures dance in his palatial mansion. He finds life's pleasures in bejewelled bowls of wine. He enjoys glamour and merriment, and has no dearth of wealth. He is handsome, and all the desires of the world dwell in his heart. Elephants sway at the entrance to his mansion; dancers intoxicated with their own beauty pirouette inside. He does not believe in God—perhaps he has never thought about God. He is not bothered about heaven or hell. Entertainment and enjoyment are his means and end. You, Shwetank, will serve this Beejgupta. Do you agree?"

"The Great Mentor's wish is my command." Shwetank's mind boggled at thought that he would understand the inner workings of this unimaginable splendour. He was keen to take the challenge.

"And Vishaldeva, you agree as well?"

"The Great Mentor's wish is my command," Vishaldeva echoed. He wanted to understand the power that Kumaragiri derived from his heady mix of youth and celibacy.

"Then let it be so," Ratnambar pronounced and stood up.

The next day, the hut was deserted. The Guru went forward into his austere domain, and the disciples into the wide world of experience.

CHAPTER ONE

Beejgupta put a bowl brimming with wine to Chitralekha's lips and said, "Chitralekha, do you know what the joy of life is?"

Chitralekha's half-open eyes were intoxicated and her cheeks rosy. She radiated ripples of beauty and the flush of youth. She sipped a draft of wine, and smiled. For a moment, her lips talked silently to Beejgupta's. Then she said, huskily, "Total freedom."

It was midnight by then. Beejgupta's mansion was lit with thousands of lamps. A soulful *shahnai* played at the doorway. Beejgupta was absorbed in youthful ardour with the city's most beautiful dancer here in his pleasure-room, while the rest of the world was enveloped in darkness.

Beejgupta burst out laughing. "I sometimes think, Chitralekha, what will be the end of youth?"

Chitralekha laughed as well, but her laugh was transient; suddenly her sweet and joyful laughing appearance turned pained and serious. Perhaps she too had sought the answer to this question in the past, but the question was so terrifying that she was not able to think about it for too long. She had felt giddy and drowned the sad thought in a bowl of wine for the time being. Hearing that question again today startled her. "A living death!" she said.

"A living death?" Beejgupta said. No, that is impossible. The end of youth is an unknown darkness, and what hides under cover of darkness I do not know, nor do I want to know. Past and future are both things of imagination, which are not relevant or meaningful. The present is what is in front of us, and that..." Beejgupta stopped. Perhaps he was searching for the right words.

"And that is happiness, and the sensuous indulgence of all the joys of the world, the essence of youth." Chitralekha completed the sentence.

Beejgupta embraced Chitralekha and said, "You intoxicate me."

"And you drive me mad," Chitralekha replied.

Chitralekha was a dancer. She was not a prostitute. In the city of Patliputra, this was not usual for an unusually beautiful dancer, but there were reasons for it, and these reasons arose from her past.

Chitralekha was widowed when she was just eighteen. At first, she had lived a life of self-control, but it did not last. One day, Krishnaditya entered her life. Krishnaditya was the son of a *kshatriya* and a *shudra*. He was a handsome young man, and he had a special attraction about him. He shattered Chitralekha's abstinence.

Chitralekha's repressed youth flourished again. The shine of her happiness overpowered the glow of her asceticism. Life took on a new meaning. Krishnaditya took a vow: "So long as we live, we will be together, no one will separate us." Chitralekha believed the vow. What followed was natural.

Chitralekha became pregnant. Her affair came out in the open. Krishnaditya's father disowned him, and Chitralekha's father expelled her. Krishnaditya, the scion of the wealthy family, embarked into a world without privileges, accompanied by a pregnant Chitralekha. The forsaken young man could not bear the insults of society for long. He preferred death. As for Chitralekha, she found shelter with a dancer. She had a son, but he died at birth.

Chitralekha's voice was sweet, and her body beautiful. Her patroness taught her classical music and dance. She became a dancer. Once again, she resolved to live an abstinent widow's life. Krishnaditya and his son had come into her life and then left her alone. Their memories were etched into her heart.

The men of Patliputra grovelled at her feet, but Chitralekha stayed true to her discipline and austerity, which gave her an angelic aura. Powerful leaders and wealthy youth thirsted for her love, but no one could get her. She appeared at communal gatherings, where her beauty lit up the scene, and then vanished like lightning. Any man who saw her once craved a second sighting.

One day Beejgupta went to see her dance. While dancing, Chitralekha's eyes met his, and her face turned pale. She felt as if Krishnaditya had descended from heaven to watch her dance. She froze, and forgetting herself and her audience, she stared fixedly at Beejgupta. Beejgupta was a young man of about twenty-five. Overpowered by Chitralekha's beauty, he returned her stunned gaze. The people in the audience turned towards the man who had attracted Chitralekha. "Ah, it's Beejgupta," they said.

Chitralekha heard their voices. She felt a pang of regret, but even more anger, at her lapse. She averted her gaze and started dancing again. After the performance Beejgupta walked up to her and said, "May I have the honour of an audience with you at your place?"

Chitralekha looked at him with a cold smile. "No, I only perform for the community. I do not entertain individuals. Individuals have no place in my life."

Beejgupta's hopes were doused by her iciness. His face fell. He summoned his courage. "Individuals make the community, don't they? The community's thirst is the sum of its members' thirsts. So why the difference?"

"If you want to know why, I'll tell you," Chitralekha said. "What people call the happiness of the community is in fact the sum of the cries of its individuals. These cries of the weak, organised by the community, can assume the form of revolution. There is no possibility of harm from the community, but the individual's attachment to the self can be a very potent source of danger."

Beejgupta had gone to seek love, not philosophy. "Do I understand then that your doors are closed to me?" he said.

A slight smile of disappointment flickered on Beejgupta's face. "The individual is the primary form of life, and the community is nothing but a group of individuals. One who prohibits discourse with individuals but seeks the community insults oneself." He turned and left, quick as an arrow.

He left, but he left a turbulence in Chitralekha's heart.

The days rolled by, and Chitralekha did not see Beejgupta again. The artificial indifference she had shown melted away, replaced by a longing for him. Each day, her eyes sought Beejgupta in the audience in her dance hall, without reward.

She tried to stifle her desire, but it grew stronger. One day, she asked a maid, "Is there a man by the name Beejgupta in the city?"

"Who does not know Beejgupta?" the maid replied. He is the most handsome young man, and a powerful courtier."

Chitralekha handed the maid a letter for Beejgupta.

The maid delivered the letter.

It read: "Chitralekha has pondered for a long time and arrived at the conclusion that only one individual can enter her life. And that individual is Beejgupta."

A tremor of pleasure coursed through Beejgupta's body. Beejgupta and Chitralekha became one that day. Still, Chitralekha was not a prostitute. Beejgupta was the only man in her life.

Beejgupta said, "Abandon and intoxication—they have always gone together, and always will. Chitralekha, how happy we are!" He laughed, and Chitralekha joined in his laughter.

At that moment, the *shahnai* stopped playing. A guard called out, "Sir, Sir, there are guests at the door. What is your command?"

Beejgupta loosened his embrace, and Chitralekha moved away. Beejgupta told a maid to accompany the guests in. He gulped down all the wine in his bowl. He wondered who it could be at that unearthly midnight hour.

Shwetank and Ratnambar entered his pleasure-house. Beejgupta hastily stood up to salute Ratnambar, and Chitralekha bowed her head as well.

Ratnambar inspected the pleasure-house at length. The scent of sandalwood, the ornate carvings, the tinkling of water, the brilliance of the lighting, the silken look of the cushions—its opulence was greater than the sum of all these. His gaze stopped at Chitralekha. "So the city's celebrated and pure dancer is at Beejgupta's pleasure house at midnight. I am surprised!" He sat on a mat spread out for him. Shwetank stood by.

"What troubles the Great Mentor to visit his servant at this time?"

Ratnambar smiled and looked straight into Beejgupta's eyes. "Beejgupta! I will be clear and to the point. You can assist me. You have been my disciple, and I have not yet taken my tribute. Today, this my pupil asked me, what is sin? I am incapable of answering his question. An ascetic's hut is not the appropriate place to understand the nature of sin. It can only be understood by being part of the senses. Your mansion and your society—Shwetank must be exposed to them. That is why I am presenting him to you as a servant. I want you to accept him as one. But remember that he can also be your brother, as you share your Guru."

"The Great Mentor's wish is my command," Beejgupta said, bowing his head.

"Well, I shall leave—I have finished one task. And, Shwetank, remember that Beejgupta is your master and you are his servant. Enjoy the splendour of your surroundings, and try to decipher the nature of sin. The good and the bad—these will present themselves to you; but do remember that good is what is good for you, and for others. And Beejgupta, please forgive Shwetank's faults. He is still inexperienced. He is taking his first steps in the adult world." With these words, Ratnambar left the pleasure house.

After Ratnambar's departure, Beejgupta looked at Shwetank attentively. "Your name is Shwetank, and you are my servant now." Beejgupta's face lit up. Pointing to Chitralekha, he asked, "Do you know, Shwetank, who this is?"

In that hour of midnight, Chitralekha's beauty was maddening under the bright lights of the pleasure-house. Shwetank was dazzled. He said, "No."

"Then listen. Her name is Chitralekha, and in spite of being the most beautiful dancer in Patliputra, she has the status of my wife. That makes her your mistress." Beejgupta chuckled. "You may be surprised, but there is nothing to be surprised about. You will learn to adapt to this life. Here, give this bowl of wine to your mistress."

Beejgupta handed a golden bowl full of fragrant wine to Shwetank.

Shwetank extended the bowl to Chitralekha. When Chitralekha took it from him, their fingers touched. The contact made Shwetank tremble. Chitralekha looked at Shwetank and said, "Young man, congratulations on entering this unfamiliar world." She drained the bowl.

At that instant, the guard announced loudly, "It is time to sleep."

Beejgupta asked Chitralekha, "Do you want to stay, or go back to your place?"

Chitralekha stood up and stepped towards the door. "I would like to go back, but I don't think I can make it alone." Her feet were unsteady.

The maid entered the pleasure-house. "Yes, it will be truly impossible for you to go alone," Beejgupta said.

After thinking for some time, he told Shwetank, "There is a chariot at the door. Help your mistress into it and escort her home. By the time you are back, your bedroom will be ready."

Shwetank went along with Chitralekha. Beejgupta ordered the maid to get Shwetank's bedroom in order, and then he found refuge with the goddess of sleep.

CHAPTER TWO

umargiri was a yogi.

Yogi?

Well, he had renounced the world.

Why?

To attain another, imaginary world with the hope that it would be full of joy. He was not interested in the common people—he dwelled on this imaginary world. He found no peace in this world, so to get peace he took refuge in solitude. He believed in control and regimentation, and he had mastered his desires.

Yogi Kumargiri had powers; but he did not believe in harnessing those powers, nor in unleashing them. His mind was stable when he was by himself. He was inclined to practise his mental exercises with total concentration in solitude. He had strengthened his body with his austere practices, but he never felt any suffering. He had baked his body, but kept himself cool by contemplating a divine bliss. Knowing that desire drives man to sin, he had suppressed his desires.

Yogi Kumargiri was at peace. He would submerge himself in an ocean of thought. He did not have the world's desires before him; he was not tormented by un-quenched thirsts. A sheath of knowledge and thought covered his inactivity. Happiness is imagined, and it brings contentment. Contentment may not have a special importance for one who has no thirst, but con-tentment ensures that the heart is not burdened with aches, and that one does not suffer from pinpricks. It is easy to indulge in the sea of imagination with a light heart devoid of sorrow. Yogi Kumargiri lived in the lap of oblivion. There is a unique pleasure in forgetting one's self and living under the delusion of imagination's live-liness. There was an imaginary thirst and an imaginary slaking of the thirst, and Kumargiri enjoyed himself at the confluence of these two forces.

And that is how Kumargiri was a yogi.

Madhupal was Kumargiri's disciple. He was famil-iar with and astonished by Kumargiri's powers.

Madhupal asked, "Master, what is the goal of self-control?"

Kumargiri sat down in controlled movements. "Peace!" he said. "And the bliss that only peace can bring.

"Change from the exterior, and emptiness from within. Change and emptiness—you will be surprised at this unlikely pairing. It is natural to ask how these two can come together. But the condition in which man rises above distinguishing between change and emptiness is the ultimate step in the ladder of enlightenment. What is this world? It is a void. And change is the movement of this void. Change is imagination and imagination itself is empty. Understand?"

Madhupal was not satisfied with this answer. "Master," he said, "you say that the world is a void. I do not understand this. How can an entity which is right in front of my eyes be void?"

Kumargiri suppressed a smile. "This is where yoga comes in. When the yogi closes his eyes, there is an indivisible vacuum, an emptiness, nothing else. Into that vacuum, happiness and sorrow, attachment and detachment, day and night, *brahma* and *maya*, all dissolve. The yogi wanders in that luminous vacuum and he is lost in it. For a few fleeting moments of his imaginary life, he reaches his origins. And salvation lies in attaining that union with *brahma* for ever. In this way, a yogi attains salvation in his life, with this very body."

Madhupal reverently bowed his head to Kumargiri's feet. He was proud of his guru's infinite wisdom, and convinced of the guru's infallibility. At this moment, Ratnambar entered Kumargiri's hut with Vishaldev.

Kumargiri rose when he saw Ratnambar before him. They embraced, and Kumargiri offered his seat to Ratnambar. "What troubles the guru to come here?"

Ratnambar spoke with his usual sincerity. "I have come to have my disciple trained under the tutelage of Kumargiri, the yogi with infinite powers."

"Master, you speak too highly of me. I am not competent to train your disciple," Kumargiri said.

"No, yogi Kumargiri, you are being magnanimous," Ratnambar said. "You are truly superior. You have risen above this world, while I am still part of it. Where logic is not enough to solve a problem, experience and imagination are needed. You have wisdom and imagination, while I have only experience. That is why I have sought you out. A person who lives with you can solve the most complex problems of life. That is why I want to make Vishaldev your disciple. Yogi Kumargiri, you will not refuse my request, and you will accept my prayer."

Kumargiri looked at Vishaldev. "Young man, what is this problem that brings you here?"

Vishaldev bowed to Kumargiri, and spoke in a serene manner: "Master, I want to know what sin is."

Kumargiri's laughter was sweet, and without malice. "You want to know what sin is? But sin can mostly be understood from experience. You cannot experience sin by living with me. Mine is the sphere of control and abstinence, and sin stays away from these two. Even so, the Great Mentor insists that I take you in as my discipline. I think it is appropriate to make it clear to you, and to the Great Mentor, that I will show you the nature of virtue, and by knowing virtue you will know sin."

"Yogi Kumargiri, you speak well," Ratnambar said. "No sensible person would object to what you said." Vishaldev sensed that Ratnambar had more to say on the subject, but had kept his counsel to himself.

"Then I accept the master's request," Kumargiri said.

Ratnambar stood up. "Very well, yogi Kumargiri, I will take your leave," he said. "You may be surprised, but

I myself do not know what sin is. After years of study and experience, I have not been able to get a complete grasp of this issue. I have entrusted my disciples to worthy people, and now I shall meditate. I will see if I can learn from worship and prayer what I could not learn from study and experience." With these words, he left.

After Ratnambar's departure, Kumargiri gestured to Vishaldev to sit down.

"Young man, you are now my disciple. I would like to ask you some questions right now. Do you know what lust is?"

"Yes," Vishaldev replied. "Lust is another name for desire."

"Right! But do you know what position lust has in a man's life? Perhaps not. That is what I shall tell you today. Lust is sin; it is the one and only means to make a life tainted. Lust motivates man to flout the laws of God, and a man drowned in lust forgets his creator, Brahma. That is why lust is despicable. If a man sets his desires aside, he can rise very high! God has three virtues: *sat*, which is the essence of being, *chit*, consciousness and *anand*, bliss. All three can be attained by a mind that is not possessed by lust. But the mind that is not free of lust is ruled by attachment, and such a mind cannot attain even one of the virtues. Vishaldev! As my disciple, your first task will be to purify your mind by giving up desire. This is a path of austerity, but not of sorrow. The proper way to give up desires is not to suppress them, but to ensure they do not form. Once a desire is born, it will grow from strength to strength. Your duty is to destroy your desires for ever. Now tell me: can you do this?"

Vishaldev had felt at home as soon as he walked in. The mud that he sat cross-legged on felt and smelled the same as back in the Great Mentor's establishment. He chose his words carefully as he replied. "Master," he said, "I will attempt this. I cannot tell whether I can do it or not. The path that you have shown me is easy, but some objections do come to my mind. Is it not against the principles of life to destroy our desires? Why is man born? To perform karma, his duty. So isn't it contrary to the will of the creator to destroy the fuel that drives man's actions? Master, I will start on the path that you have directed me to, the moment you help clear my confused mind."

Kumargiri was prepared for this answer. He said, "Vishaldev, you speak well, because you are also influenced by one mentor. I will have to wean you away from that influence. I will remove your confusion, but not today. A deluded guru's disciples will harbour some wrong notions, but, Vishaldev, I sense that Ratnambar's thoughts lean towards atheism. I am a believer. Before you learn anything from me, you will have to accept two hypotheses. The first is that Brahma, the creator, exists, and the second is that duty is the primary aspect of life."

"Master, I accept these," Vishaldev said.

Kumargiri stood up and said, "Then I am at ease. I will teach you, and guide you towards the path of freedom, and in this process, you shall understand the nature of sin."

CHAPTER THREE

hwetank was celibate. His sphere was that of study, shorn of experience, and his goal was to acquire knowledge. He was twenty-five, and by this age he had studied the philosophies of various schools, and the codes of conduct laid down by seers. He had read grammar and literature. He had read the poets who wrote of love and romance, and tried to understand them as well, but failed. He had not known the intoxication that comes from loving a woman.

The celibate Shwetank and the alluring Chitralekha—Beejgupta introduced them to each other light-heartedly; when he dwelled on the circumstances, he found them curious. An ascetic and a dancer. He smiled to himself at this pairing.

What Beejgupta found amusing, Shwetank found troubling. Almost every night, Shwetank had to escort Chitralekha home. Each time he did so, Chitralekha would be intoxicated. The abandon in her eyes caused tremors in his heart. Woman and wine—the combination was like a lamp around which Shwetank hovered, helpless, like a moth. Shwetank would look at Chitralekha and feel a strange joy; what was this joy? It was a tremor of an unknown passion. When Chitralekha's drowsy, sensual eyes met Shwetank's, he swayed like a man possessed.

In Beejgupta's mansion, Shwetank came to be looked upon as a younger brother. Beejgupta's servants did not consider him as one of their own. Instead, they treated him like a master. Shwetank had access to all the material pleasures of the affluent, and he was introduced to the influential people of the city. He had been ejected from pitch darkness and into a brightly lit world, one that he found hard to believe that he was in. He struggled to adapt to this new world. He realised that he was in the real world now, in the thick of virtue and sin. Desires enmeshed him on all sides. He was carried on the waves of the daily life of this world.

One day, Beejgupta travelled out of the city. His departure was urgent and sudden, and he would return by evening. Chitralekha's chariot drew up at the gate at her usual time. Shwetank welcomed Chitralekha in Beejgupta's pleasure house.

They sat down, and Chitralekha asked him, "Where is your master?"

"Where is your master?" the question echoed in Shwetank's mind, and it hurt him. It pierced him like an arrow. Had he heard the question from another, ordinary, woman, he might have just minded it a bit, or retorted fiercely. But Shwetank realised his position and his insignificance for the first time, and felt a pang of regret. He suppressed these feelings and replied, "Mistress, he has gone out to work."

Chitralekha asked, "When will he be back?"

"Any time now," Shwetank said.

"Shwetank, I am thirsty!"

Shwetank stood up. He had realised his position, and Beejgupta's words rang in his mind: "Remember Chitralekha is your mistress". He took her cold water in a gold tumbler.

Chitralekha looked at the water and chuckled. "Shwetank, you are just a child."

Shwetank detected her sarcasm, but he was puzzled. "What did I do wrong, mistress?" he asked.

This time Chitralekha laughed aloud. "Shwetank, you do not understand. Thirst should not be quenched. Fire does not need water. It needs *ghee* to stoke it. Life is an unquenched thirst, and to quench this thirst it is to extinguish life. I have no need of water; I want wine."

Shwetank was stunned by this reply. It terrified him, but it was logical. He laughed as well, and said, "Perhaps I should become a disciple of Patliputra's most beautiful woman." He placed a bowl of wine before her.

Chitralekha gulped the wine and put the bowl in front of Shwetank. She had a bolster by her side. Her head-cloth slipped. A string of pearls glittered against her hair, which was black like the darkness of the night. How beautiful she was—Shwetank had never even imagined such incomparable beauty. He had to use all his powers to stop himself from tracing the lines of her form. Chitralekha's was an intoxicating image of youth. Her rosy cheeks were flushed. Her lips lit up her face with a smile, and her eyes danced with pleasure.

Shwetank stared at her quietly. She said, "I see you don't drink, Shwetank. I put the wine bowl right in front of you, but your hands dare not raise it to your lips. Let me ask you a question. You must tell me the truth."

Shwetank bowed his head.

"You have been celibate," she said. "Your guru must have prohibited wine. Why?"

Shwetank spoke softly: "Mistress, self-control is an essential part of life, and wine and self-control are enemies."

"And what is the objective of self-control?"

"Joy and peace."

Chitralekha raised the bowl to her lips and asked, "And the goal of life?"

Chitralekha's eyes had reddened with intoxication. Shwetank felt a kind of music in her voice and poetry in her words. "The goal of life?" he said. "Joy and peace."

"That's where you are wrong, young man!" Chitralekha said. "Joy is fulfilment, peace is inaction, but the essence of life is constant action and unfulfilled thirst. Life is turbulent; it is about change. There is no place for joy and peace in life." She placed the rim of the wine bowl against Shwetank's lips.

Shwetank considered removing the bowl, but Chitralekha's eyes were enchanting. He found himself powerless to resist her. The wine flowed down his throat.

At that very moment, from behind, Beejgupta chortled and said, "Ascetic! The dancer has initiated you well today! I congratulate Chitralekha."

Shwetank was startled out of his enchanted daze. He felt crestfallen. He looked at Chitralekha, and then at Beejgupta, and bowed his head. After Beejgupta had left, he said to Chitralekha, "Mistress, today you shattered my asceticism. Why did you do this? You have ignited a flame in my heart. Why? Why did you come into my life like a thunderstorm?" He held Chitralekha's hands tightly.

Chitralekha replied with a smile. "Shwetank, you are mistaken. What you call asceticism is just destroying the soul. I have only shown you that being intoxicated is a prime part of life. As for igniting a flame in your heart, I have just shown you the real meaning of life." Chitralekha turned serious. She pushed aside Shwetank's hand. "Shwetank, do remember that it is impossible for me to enter your life. I know myself too well. I love only one person in the world, and that is Beejgupta. Do not even imagine that I can be a part of your life. Now you are free to go."

Shwetank turned pale. He had lost to a dancer—in knowledge, in duty and in personality. "As you command, mistress," he said. The crushed and insulted ascetic moved towards the door.

Chitralekha thought for a while, and called out to Shwetank after he had crossed the doorway, "Shwetank, stop. I have more to say to you. Come back."

Shwetank stopped. He did not return, but he turned around and replied, "Mistress, do you have more

words to reprimand me with? Have I not got enough reward for the weakness of my soul? Madam, you are my
mistress and also my life…no, excuse me, you are only
my mistress. Your wish is my command. What is your
wish?" His eyes turned watery.

Chitralekha heard Shwetank—the child Shwetank—
and felt a pang of regret. She said, "Shwetank! I did you
wrong. Forgive me for being cruel. I feel an affection for
you. You are like a brother. I share your sorrow. I have
perhaps insulted you unknowingly, and I ask you to forgive me for that."

Chitralekha's apology melted Shwetank. The pain
in his heart melted like ice. He saw the image of a goddess in Chitralekha, and sensed a divine aura around
her. He felt she was not just a dancer; he felt a deep spiritual bond with her. He said, "Mistress, there is no need
to ask for forgiveness. It was my mistake, and I am the
one who should be punished, but, mistress, you have
showered me with mercy instead. You have saved me
from sinking, and I am indebted to you beyond words.
It is you who must forgive me."

With that, he walked out of the house, leaving Chitralekha standing still. She felt remorseful that she had
made an innocent young boy fall for her charms, without meaning to.

Shwetank went straight to Beejgupta. He fell at
Beejgupta's feet, and simply said, "Master, punish me."

Beejgupta was startled. He raised Shwetank, and
asked, "Shwetank, why? What is the matter?"

Shwetank spoke in a hoarse voice. "Master, I have
betrayed you. I am guilty of loving the woman who

loves you and whom you love; the woman who is my mistress."

Beejgupta understood what had happened, but he did not betray any emotion. "Shwetank, how do you know that she loves me?"

"She herself told me," Shwetank said. The wine had affected him. He felt a kind of vigour coursing through him. "Today I let go of self-control by taking wine from her hands, and that happened because I fell in love with her."

Beejgupta pretended to be serious. "Shwetank! What if she had not told you that she loves me, and she had offered herself to you? What would you have done?"

Shwetank pondered this for a while. He said, "Perhaps I would have not even asked my master for forgiveness, and I would have betrayed my master and committed the ultimate crime against my guru."

Beejgupta patted Shwetank's back. He said, "Shwetank, there is no need to ask for my forgiveness. What you did was natural; every man in your situation would have done it. What you did was right, and what you would have done would also have been right. You would not have the slightest blame to bear. What happened would have flown from the circumstances. But I am happy for you. You did sin against someone, but by owning up to that person you washed your sin away. You told me the truth, as you should have done. As for the purported betrayal, Shwetank, there you are mistaken. You have just entered the world of the senses. You lack the experiences of this world. You will have to pass many tests of experience, and distinguish between duty and sin. Desires will take on strong forms and torment you, and you will have to conquer them. Your powers will be tested. The arena of victory and defeat is in that world, not in the wilderness."

Shwetank was crying. "Master, I shall do all this. But I should still be punished," he said.

Beejgupta put a hand on Shwetank's head, and said, "Why do you cry? You want to be punished for a crime—but you did no crime. Crime is in the act, not in the thought. The thought is just a means for action. If you still want punishment, I will give you the hardest one. You will escort Chitralekha to her mansion, as usual."

CHAPTER FOUR

ishaldeva saw a great soul in his teacher Kumargiri. He bowed before Kumargiri's knowledge and vigour. Kumargiri's arguments were infallible; he could cast away Vishaldeva's doubts in seconds. Kumargiri initiated Vishaldeva into the practice of yoga. Kumargiri got a worthy disciple and Vishaldeva a worthy guru.

One day, Kumargiri was teaching Vishaldeva about the role of worship. The sun had set, and the flame of an earthen lamp flickered in the dark hut. A footstep at the door intruded into the sounds of the forest, and a voice called out, "Two lost travellers need shelter for a night."

Kumargiri replied, "They are welcome. My hut is open to every lost creature."

A man and a woman entered the hut.

Kumargiri was startled to see the woman. "Why did you not mention that you have a woman with you?

Do you not know that this hut belongs to a yogi who has renounced the world of the senses?"

"Sir," the man replied, "I do know that this is a yogi's hut, but I did not think that this yogi who has conquered his senses would hesitate to provide shelter to a woman for a night, especially a woman accompanied by a man.

Kumargiri's face lost its lustre. By that time, the woman had seated herself on mat, and her face was lit by the dim light of the lamp. "My guest, I hesitated to have a woman in the hut because woman is darkness, attachment, delusion and lust. There is no place for woman in my enlightened world. Still, you both are my guests, and it is my duty to serve you both."

The woman heard out the conversation. When Kumargiri finished, she said "This darkness salutes the moth entranced by light."

Her words were sharp and deadly as an arrow, her voice soft and lyrical. She was statuesque and poised, and she had the assurance of a woman who enjoyed her sensuousness. Kumargiri was surprised by this unique salutation from a unique woman, and he looked at her carefully. He was nonplussed. He had never seen a woman so beautiful. He chose not to reply to the woman. He said to the man, "I have the right to be introduced to my guests."

The man replied, "Sir, this servant is called Beejgupta, and he is a courtier of Patliputra, and this lady, Chitralekha, is the most beautiful dancer of the city."

"Beejgupta and Chitralekha!" Kumargiri now turned to Chitralekha. "Dancer Chitralekha, a veil of abandon sheaths the cruelty of your poetic speech. Your beauty hides the venom inside you. You are my guest, and you have greeted me. It is my duty to bless you. May god grant you the gift of good thought."

Chitralekha's laugh filled the hut. Her laughter had an enchanting quality. "Yogi," she said, "good thought has different connotations—the joy of attachment is the sorrow of dispassion. One sets a code of conduct for oneself and believes in it. Each one thinks he is on the right path, and those who follow a different code are on the wrong path."

The dancer, slave of attachment, faced the yogi, master of detachment. Mutiny and peace, life and nirvana faced off against each other.

Kumargiri spoke without a tremor: "There is but one truth, the knowledge of reality. And that is the right path, the one that leads to peace and joy." Kumargiri's tone was grave, and his years of meditation gave a sheen to the youthful skin of the handsome yogi. His wide eyes had the light of peace.

The yogi's eyes locked with the dancer's for a moment. Desire trembled before austerity. Chitralekha sensed that she was seated in front of a true and great yogi. She willed herself to say, "Peace and joy! Peace is another name for inaction, and as far as joy is concerned, it has no single definition."

Yogi Kumargiri was dumbfounded at Chitralekha's logical distortion of the principles of philosophy. He realised that the woman he was talking to was as wise as she was beautiful. She had the gift of original thought, and she was intelligent.

Kumargiri was silent for some time. After a while, he said in a firm tone, "You are right, lady. Peace is another name for inaction. And inaction brings freedom. What the world sees as inaction is actually far from it, because in that condition it is the mind that works. What this inaction means is a merging with the void that we are all born from, and that void is the pre-destined goal of life. And as for your comment about the definition of joy, I agree with you. But there is only one joy. When one realises what that joy is, one is uplifted well above the ordinary circumstances of life."

Chitralekha saw meaning in Kumargiri's words. She felt herself drawn to the young yogi without willing herself in that direction. She summoned her courage again. "Void!" she said. "Yogi, who believes in that void? What is in front of us—that is the truth, and it is eternal. Your void is a figment of the imagination. You, who uphold the greatness of the void, do you see any difference between your attachment to it, and my attachment to mine-ness? If you do, you do not believe in the void. If you don't, your distinctions between knowledge and darkness, joy and sorrow, woman and man, sin and virtue are false. God created man to act in the world, not to turn away from its difficulties like a coward. Oh, and joy—joy is another name for satiation. And satiation is only feasible where there is desire, where there is lust."

The yogi's expression was serious; the dancer smiled. Beejgupta was enchanted by this exposition of his life's principles by his life-partner and disciple. She looked divine in that dim light that accentuated her curves. He noticed Vishaldeva's raised eyebrows—the boy was obviously stunned at the dancer's knowledge and her articulation. Both waited for Kumargiri's reply.

Kumargiri stayed mute for a while. When he spoke, it was with gravity. "God and man are one. The difference is outer-worldly. Attachment is born from the union of *maya* and *brahma*, and *maya* is a part of *brahma* though it seems separate. The *brahma* is trapped in the world of the senses as long as it is engrossed with *maya*. Only after abandoning *maya* does the *brahma* become its true self. You and I—we are not really very different. Like you, I am part of *brahma*. The small difference is that I have given up *maya* and you have not. I keep *maya* separate from my life, so that I do not move backward. About joy being synonymous with satiation, there too you are mistaken. If satiation is the only means to contentment, then satiation is definitely joy, but your joy then leads to being ensnared in the bonds of the world and does not help to attain satisfaction. *Brahma* united with *maya* will always flounder in the web of worldly actions. It is the act of leaving *maya* that empowers the *brahma* to know itself, and find satiation, satisfaction and contentment. Joy is the abandonment of this sorrowful world."

Kumargiri was quiet for a while. Then, without giving Chitralekha an opportunity to reply, he continued, "And remember this—there is no end to argument. Truth lies in experience. It is impossible to be enlightened without experience and belief." He stood up. "It is late. We had better rest."

Chitralekha was not satisfied with this answer, and Kumargiri sensed that. But Kumargiri had attracted

Chitralekha. The yogi saw knowledge in the dancer, and the dancer saw beauty in the yogi. It was strange—they were dissatisfied with each other; they were also impressed by each other. Both sensed a pull—the yogi of knowledge and the dancer of beauty. What Beejgupta saw, he could not fathom. The conversation had created an unease in his heart. The unease was not about any principle. So, what was it about? He could not put a finger on it. In his heart of hearts, he knew that Chitralekha's attraction to Kumargiri had cast a shadow on him, but he did not want to believe it.

"My disciple Vishaldeva will rest in my hut tonight," Kumargiri said. "His hut is available. My guests can retire there."

Beejgupta stood up, and Chitralekha followed him. As she walked away, Chitralekha said, "Yogi! Austerity is a waste of life. Austerity has one goal—the destruction of the self. The dancer Chitralekha bows before your holy feet." With a friendly chuckle, she left the hut.

Kumargiri sighed and smiled, after she had left. "That's right! Austerity is the destruction of the Self, and the Self is the union of *brahma* and *maya*. When the Self destructs, the flow of *maya* trickles off, and what is left is *sat*, existence, *chit*, consciousness, *anand*, bliss—the constituents of the *brahma*. But dancer, if you had experience, if your circumstances were different, you would also know this. You have knowledge but you lack someone to show you direction. I pity you."

Vishaldeva showed Beejgupta and Chitralekha the way to the door of his hut.

Before   sleeping,   Beejgupta   whispered,
"Chitralekha?"

"Yes, dearest?" Chitralekha said.

Beejgupta took a deep breath and said, "I feel a
heaviness in my heart. I sense clouds of sorrow over the
horizon. Kumargiri is a yogi…and perhaps he has the
power to attract, too?"

Chitralekha grew pale for a moment, but she gathered herself and said, "Dearest, Kumargiri is a yogi, and
a fool, to boot. His soul is dead."

Chitralekha tried to deceive Beejgupta, and herself. She spoke again: "Kumargiri lives in the wilderness,
and you and I are the actors of the real world of actions
and reactions. Kumargiri has conquered desire, but we
believe in it. Kumargiri's goal in life is the imaginary
void, while ours is fun! Dearest, no one in this world
can come between us."

Beejgupta face lit up with joy. "Amen!" he said.

Chitralekha had deceived Beejgupta, but not herself. "But Kumargiri is definitely handsome," she said to
herself.

Chapter Five

vast courtyard of Emperor Chandragupta's palace was fragrant with the incense-laden smoke from a great *yagya*, a prayer ceremony for the emperor's well-being. The emperor sat on a jewelled gold throne, facing east, and his guests filled the courtyard. To his right, the invited nobles sat in order of seniority, and on his left the chief officers of his government. In front were the intellectuals—the *brahmans*, who controlled rituals, and ascetic sages.

In keeping with tradition, the assembly was organised for a philosophical debate. Emperor Chandragupta addressed his Chief Minister, Chanakya, the renowned strategist who had shaped the foundation of the Maurya empire. "Minister, master of policy, your principles of governance sometimes overlook religious norms. Why these compromises? Can you kindly tell us whether the principles of governance are subject to those of religion or not?"

Chanakya stood up, bowed first to the gathering of intellectuals and then to the Emperor, and took his seat. "The Emperor is right," he said. "My principles of governance sometimes go against the obscurantist principles of religion. That is clear and I acknowledge it. At the same time, I have to say that religion is manufactured by society. Religion has not given birth to moral policy—on the contrary, it is morality that has given birth to religion. Policy consists of the rules made by society for its survival, and logic is the basis for policy, which reflects in the principles of governance. Religion is based on belief, and it is useful for society to bind each individual in a bondage of belief and trust, and to make him follow its rules. At times, circumstances may force society to go against religion in the interest if its people. So slowly the norms of religion change."

Chanakya's statement was greeted by a stunned silence from the intellectuals. The Emperor looked with pride at his minister, and then at the intellectuals. The minister had made a provocative statement, and his words carried the ring of credibility; but what he had said was also unusual. Who would answer Chanakya? The assembly waited.

A young yogi spoke up calmly from the rows of the intellectuals. "King! God created man and man formed society. *Dharma*, religion, is God's worldly form, a means of uniting man with God. To ignore religion is to ignore God, and it implies distancing oneself from the truth. There is one truth, and religion is another name

for it. Policy that goes against religious is not princi-
pled, it is unprincipled. Right and wrong, justice and
injustice—religion provides the criteria, and the whole
world falls under the scope of religion."

The venerable Chanakya looked at the young
yogi who had spoken—it was Kumargiri—like a giant
demon would eye a dwarf. He said, "You, who flaunt
the superiority of religion, do you know who created
religion?"

"God himself, working through man's inner self."

"And who created God?"

The assembly was shocked at the question. "Who
created God?" There was a tremor in the crowd.

"God has no beginning," Kumargiri spoke in the
same calm manner as before.

"You are right, yogi. God has no beginning. This
is not new. Every one says that God has no beginning.
Does anyone seated here know God?" Chanakya's voice
was raised and his eyes fiery. Without waiting for a response, he added, "Yes, god has no beginning and God
is eternal, but I can state with confidence that no one
knows that God. He is beyond imagination. He is truth;
he is so incandescent that no human can open his eyes
in God's presence. Try to attain that truth, meditate and
practise the harshest austerity to reach God; you will
fail. If you can know God, creator of the indivisible and
the infinite, what kind of God is he? But yogi, my god
and yours, the God we pray to, is different from that almighty God. Our God is imaginary. Society has created
him to fulfil our needs."

Chanakya paused and looked around him. He was greeted with pin-drop silence. Yogi Kumargiri's eyes were closed as if he was absorbed in deep thought. Chanakya stood up and looked at the intellectuals and scholars again, as if daring them to challenge him. He exuded confidence. After waiting a while for an answer, he said, "I have not finished! Yes, I said that your god and mine, whom we worship, is a figment of the imagination and a creation of society. This God has several forms. Now let us turn to the inner self. Here, again, our conventional wisdom is flawed. The inner self is not created by God; it is created by society. If it was actually a gift of God, humans of different societies would not have different inner selves. If it is really the one God who has framed the rules of religion, the same rules would apply to every individual. But that is not how it is. Individuals in different societies differ in their inner selves. One's conscience abhors what one's society abhors. It follows that the inner self, the conscience, is created by society. Our inner self is nothing but our complete and blind faith in society's rules. It does not have an existence independent of society."

Chanakya sat down. Many of the intellectuals, moved by his indisputable logic, bowed to him.

It was not clear whether Kumargiri heard Chanakya or not. His eyes were closed, and his serene face had an other-wordly glow. He was absorbed in his thoughts, but Chanakya had won the argument. The consensus among the assembly was that Kumargiri had not been able to counter Chanakya's arguments.

The Emperor was smiling. After waiting for some time, he stood and said, "The debate is over. It is time for a dance." He gestured to one of his companions. The silence was broken as the courtiers cheered.

Chitralekha entered the assembly from her make-up room. The tinkle of her ornaments created a melody of their own. Her entry electrified the assembly, some of whose members had found the debate dry and boring. It was as if the red morning sun had pierced the faint light of dawn, or cold winter air had been swept away by a fragrant spring breeze.

From the centre of the courtyard, Chitralekha first saluted the Emperor. Her beauty stunned the audience. Her face lit up the hall like a full moon, and her plait was like the mythological serpent that, tormented by its own venom, clung to the moon to snatch its nectar. The pearls intertwined in her hair glittered like the stars, that had lined up to attack the serpent when they saw it approach the moon. The fine silken head-cloth she wore was as good as transparent. Her well-formed breasts seemed to glow through her thin, gold-embroidered, silken blouse. Her long skirt had golden threads that glittered in the brightly lit night. Bedecked with jewelled ornaments, she looked like Goddess Lakshmi personified. When she turned to the courtiers and smiled at them, their zealous murmurs filled the assembly. After gracing every one of them with a fleeting glimpse, she stopped at Beejgupta. Her smile spread from her lips to her eyes. Beejgupta answered her greeting with a silent, but eloquent, reply.

Chitralekha then bowed her head to the wise men. As she was turning away from their direction, her gaze fell on Kumargiri. She was arrested by the young yogi. For a moment, she waited for Kumargiri to look at her; the yogi was still lost in a world of his own. Disappointed, Chitralekha turned away.

The *sarangi* joined the grave beat of the *mridang* and the notes of *raaga kalyan* filled the air. The tremor of happiness that Chitralekha's entry had created heightened as Chitralekha's feet, delicate as lotus flowers, started dancing, the bells on her feet accentuating the music. Her form shimmered, and the beat of the *mridang* was like the rumbling of storm clouds. The audience watched in an engrossed silence.

Suddenly, Kumargiri opened his eyes. They exuded a divine light. He stood erect, and said gravely, "Minister Chanakya! I know God and to satisfy you and this assembly I can show him to you right now."

The trance was broken for many in the audience. Some people actually heard Kumargiri; a few did not. Among those who did not, the majority were young nobles who were enthralled by the dance. They shouted, "Get that yogi to sit down!"

Chitralekha did not hear Kumargiri either. She was too absorbed in her dance. She displayed her unrivalled skill as her feet played out their magical rhythm. The Emperor cast a meaningful glance at Chanakya, who acknowledged it with a barely perceptible nod.

Chanakya rose to his feet and said, "Nobles and wise men, yogi Kumargiri claims that he knows God and can show God's presence to all of us, here and now.

The Emperor has given his assent. Let us suspend the dance for some time."

This time the nobles heard each word, and so did Chitralekha. She stopped herself and looked first at Chanakya with anger, and then with double the anger at Kumargiri. Then she quietly stepped away to a corner.

Chanakya said, "Yogi Kumargiri, we are all ready to see God."

Kumargiri gave up his seat. As he stood up and took centre stage, a tense stillness fell over the crowd. He closed his eyes for a while, and then said, "Pandits and courtiers, look at me!"

Near where he stood, a flame shot up from the altar of the *yagya* and moved towards the ceiling. It shone brighter than the mid-day summer sun. It touched the roof and pierced it. Slowly, it widened and its light became so intense that it blinded the audience. The surprising thing was that the flame had no heat; it only dazzled with its incandescence. Kumargiri said, "This is true."

Chanakya shouted, "Yogi, you lie! There is nothing!"

This time the astonished people looked at Chanakya. Kumargiri said, "Does the venerable Minister not see the light of truth?"

Chanakya again said, "What light? I see nothing."

Kumargiri did not argue. He said, "Look again."

This time the flame dimmed and transformed into a circle of light. From that halo, the stunned onlookers saw many creatures emerge from one side and submerge into the other. They saw huge cities being build and destroyed in it. They saw earth, water, fire and sky in it. Slowly, all those visuals disappeared, and only the circle of light remained.

Yogi Kumargiri spoke softly, "And this is God."

Chanakya shouted like a madman. "I see nothing! I have to say you are lying! This assembly is my witness—they will tell you."

The assembly spoke in one voice: "The Minister is wrong. We have seen the light!"

The Chief Minister, stunned, looked at Emperor Chandragupta, who gently said, "Minister, Kumargiri does not lie. We have seen the truth and God."

"My eyes deceived me for the first time. Young yogi! You win, and I lose," Chanakya said and sat down.

Kumargiri had just taken a few steps away from the gathering when he heard Chitralekha speak out, "Yogi! Stop! I have a few questions."

The people turned to her, their curiosity aroused beyond measure. Kumargiri had to stop. Chitralekha came forward and said, "Yogi, whatever you showed, I did not see either. The others here can all say that the Chief Minister lied, but I won't. In the name of Truth and the Almighty, I ask you—have you really seen the form of God that you showed before this assembly tonight?"

The dancer's eyes met the yogi's. The yogi's eyes glowed with the power of belief and the energy that comes from meditation; The dancer's eyes had the shine of excitement and the glow of disbelief. Kumargiri abruptly said, "No!"

A murmur ran through the crowd. Chanakya stood up, his face lit up with joy, but Chitralekha ignored him. "Yogi!" she said. "Is it not correct that you used the power of your inner self to influence this gathering? Is that which you have shown them the true form of God manufactured by your imagination? Do not lie; I ask you this question in the name of God and truth. And remember you are a yogi."

Kumargiri pondered for a while, and said, "You are right."

The audience was stunned. Chitralekha went on, "I have another question. Is it also true that you can not show the things that you imagine to people who have mastered their inner self to the extent that their mastery of the self is stronger than yours?

The assembly stirred with unease. Kumargiri realised he was close to being outwitted. He thought for a moment, and replied with equanimity. "The one who believes in God has power over his self. An atheist does not have it. If one has imagination, it will surely be influenced, but if one's imagination is dead—suffocated by the black cloth of atheism—one cannot know God. Those who did not see God this time have had their imagination strangled. They are atheists and atheists can never see God."

Chanakya looked at the Emperor, and the Emperor made a hidden signal to him. Chanakya stepped forward and placed a crown on Chitralekha's head. "Dancer Chitralekha," he said, "you win today. You brought out the hidden truth that yogi Kumargiri tried to shroud with his use of his will power." He turned to

Kumargiri. "And yogi, you were wrong to act as you did. You should be punished, but the right to punish you rests with Chitralekha."

Kumargiri's eyes reddened with anger. "No one in this assembly can defeat me, or punish me!" he stood erect.

The people shrank back in fear at Kumargiri's enraged expression, but Chitralekha laughed. Smiling, she advanced towards the yogi—the crowd was now buzzing. Chitralekha gestured to the musicians. "Yogi!" she said. "I have been awarded the right to punish you, and I am bent on exercising this right. See how I dare to punish you." She took the golden crown from her head, and placed it on Kumargiri's.

The *sarangi* and *mridang* started their melody at that instant, and Chitralekha, resplendent in her glamour, danced with fluid movements. The audience cheered in applause.

Kumargiri stood stunned. He recovered when Chitralekha danced away from him, and his ears registered the ringing applause. "Punishment and defeat—I will have to think about these," he said. His words were drowned out and he walked away from the crowd.

Chapter Six

he yogi was not used to being trampled on. It was a new experience for him. Its intensity drained him. He had never imagined that he could be defeated—and to be defeated by a woman! And what a woman: an ordinary dancer. He analysed his situation with a troubled heart. He had snatched defeat from the jaws of victory. He had triumphed over the Emperor's chosen wise men. He had lost to darkness. It was natural to lose to darkness. Great spiritual seekers had been defeated by women; but they had lost to the woman's allure, and not to the woman's knowledge. Kumargiri's predicament was unique.

Victory and defeat—these are natural. But this defeat was unusual. Perhaps the woman had not defeated him in the sphere of knowledge. She had triumphed with her magnanimity. The crown of victory was still on his head. He remembered it now, and he grabbed it and flung it to the ground. His thought pummelled him again. "Defeat!" The word was not even in his vocabulary. He had renounced worldly pleasures for victory. He had gone through intense austerity for victory. Why this defeat? "No!" he said to himself. "Defeat is not acceptable. I cannot be defeated. Will my long years of spiritual seeking end in this ignominious way? Never!"

His eyes fell on the golden crown lying in the dust. He looked at it for some time with a fixed gaze. It seemed to say, "Yogi, you did not lose. You won." A shiver ran through him. Slowly, he inched towards it. He stopped when he reached it. "A defeat tinged with victory! What a strange mix. Do I have any claim on this trophy? I was publicly trounced by the woman; she was crowned. She handed it down to me." Kumargiri turned his face away. He willed himself to walk away, but his feet did not obey him. The crown lay there, its glimmer enhanced in the silvery light of the moon. "But how did I get it? If the anointed victor acknowledged her defeat at my hands, whose victory is it? Mine. Dancer, you accepted defeat—why?"

"Because you won me over."

The yogi was startled. Chitralekha stood in front of him, with her face lit up by a sweet smile and her eyes dancing with merriment. "Yogi," she said. "It is strange that the loser is elated and the winner restless."

Kumargiri did not say a word. He looked at the crown.

"What's this? The crown lies on the ground. Yogi, do you not accept your victory?" Chitralekha's smile disappeared.

It was a difficult question. It was hard for the self-respecting yogi to deny victory or accept defeat. He stayed silent.

Chitralekha bent and picked up the crown. "Enlightened yogi, it is impossible for me to defeat you." She put the crown on his head. Kumargiri did not resist. His eyes were closed and he was lost in thought.

"What are you thinking?"

This time Kumargiri opened his eyes. "Dancer Chitralekha," he said, "in fact you think you have defeated me. And that is why you insult me again and again. But you are wrong and what you are trying will not work. This yogi has abandoned the world, and he has no concept of esteem. All that you are doing is in vain."

Chitralekha replied calmly. "Yogi, you could not be more wrong. I repeat again: I do not have the power or the energy to defeat you."

Kumargiri stared at Chitralekha, at this strange woman whose pale face flushed red as he looked at her with his unflinching gaze. All of a sudden, a tremor passed through his still body. He clasped Chitralekha's hand in a tight grip, and said, "Dancer, tell me the truth! Why did you come here like a shadow? What makes you embarrass me?"

His body was now trembling with excitement. Chitralekha stood very close to him. Her languid, intoxicating eyes locked with his.

In the fragrant spring, with its breeze laden with life, the moonlight danced in merriment and the stars smiled. In that lonely place, on that quiet night, the alluring Chitralekha stood before Kumargiri. She smiled and replied, "I have come seeking an initiation into spirituality from the one who conquered me."

Kumargiri excitement abated. "Beautiful one, have you even thought about the meaning of being initiated by me?"

Chitralekha was earnest and animated. "Yes, I have—not once, but many times."

Kumargiri willed his eyes away from the extraordinarily beauty. "No, you do not understand the significance of what we are discussing. My initiation means forsaking all of the pleasures and desires of the world, accepting the inaction that you detest, and putting your delicate body through the emotionless spiritual seeking that you once mocked."

Chitralekha pondered this for a while. In spite of being a dancer, and an opponent of philosophy, she was not used to lying. Her soul shouted, "No!" Her heart instigated her to say "Yes". Her heart won out. It tricked her into telling the biggest lie of her life. "Yogi, I am ready for all this," she said.

"You are ready?" Kumargiri was stunned. "Beautiful one, you are making a big mistake. What you have set out to do is very difficult. It is not for everyone. Do you have any idea how hard it is to be liberated from mine-ness and attachment? You will not be able to do it."

Chitralekha became serious. "You are right," she said. "It is difficult. But it is not impossible."

Kumargiri looked at Chitralekha from head to toe. She was still dressed in the attire she had performed in, and she exuded the same radiance and voluptuousness.

Her eyes danced with excitement. Kumargiri, who had never paid any attention to a woman's beauty, who was above love and lust, said to himself, "This woman is an extraordinary beauty." A slight tremor rocked him. For the first time, this tremor gave the yogi a sense of earthly delight. How strange it was! He said, "Beautiful one, I will have to think about how appropriate it is to initiate you. I cannot take a view on it now."

"You cannot take a view on it now, yogi?" Chitralekha repeated the words. "Why? Do you not believe in yourself? Or do you not have faith in me? Remember this: initiating me into the spiritual path may not mean much for you, but for me it is a matter of life and death. If one has water, refuses to give it to a parched guest who craves it, and stands by while the guest is in the throes of death, one incurs a terrible sin. His soul will never find peace."

Kumargiri shrank back at this answer. "Beautiful lady, let me be honest with you," he said. "I hesitate to give you the initiation that you want because your distorted principles of philosophy have grown deep roots in your mind. These distorted principles give you the strength to argue with sharp logic, and with great effect. I am scared that instead of rooting out those distortions from your mind, I myself will be snared in them…" Kumargiri stopped himself. "No, I won't be able to take it." He had realised his intellectual weakness for the first time, and blurted it out as well. Unfortunately, he had shown this weakness to a dancer. He was furious with himself. His face reddened. "Beautiful one, what I just said is irrelevant. I now have only one request for

you—please just go away. Grant me some time to pon-
der over all this."

"Very well, yogi!" Chitralekha said. "If my presence
makes you unhappy, then it is just as well that I go away.
You must be thinking that the woman in front of you
is a dancer, the representative of illusion, of darkness.
You are afraid of my distorted principles, but your fear
has no basis. The moment I started out to get initiation
from you, I had left all my beliefs behind. You have told
me that you think of woman as a force of darkness and
delusion—all I can say is that you are mistaken. Woman
is energy! She is a force of creation if her companion is
worthy, and a force of destruction if the companion is
unworthy. A man who fears women is either unworthy
or a coward. And the unworthy and the cowardly one
can never be a complete man."

Chitralekha walked away, and stopped after a few
steps. Kumargiri's gaze was fixed on a distance horizon.
"Oh, and one more thing. I will come here again tomorrow. I am giving you ample time to think this over. If
you think it appropriate to initiate me, let me know tomorrow. This servant salutes your pious feet."

Kumargiri saw Chitralekha departing. He was
troubled by his reaction to her presence, the quicken-
ing of his breath, the loss of composure. Her melodious
words echoed in his ears. His eyes imagined her dancing
in all her glamour. He felt possessed, like an in-satiated
drinker scared of falling unconscious while scented
wine trickles into the dust in front of him. He could not
stop himself from calling out, "Stop, beautiful lady!"

His eyes lowered themselves. His soul revolted against his leaping heart, but the heart parried the soul's chiding by saying, "I must clarify my position by answering this woman's questions." Chitralekha turned back with hope on her face and a flutter in her heart.

"Yogi, perhaps you realised your mistake. What do you say now?"

Kumargiri stood silent. His eyes feasted on Chitralekha's beauty in the moonlight. He noticed how her delicate make-up emphasised her natural beauty. He found her intoxicating. He felt overcome by desire, and he enjoyed the sensation. Suddenly, questions arose in his mind: "What is woman? What is beauty? Why did the creator make these things?" These questions were not justified. His thoughts, honed by years of concentration, prodded him—was he straying from his chosen path? He made a supreme effort to suppress these conflicting thoughts.

"Beautiful one, which mistake? I do not know of any mistake," he said.

Chitralekha did not think it right to argue. "Revered one, forgive me. The one whom I want to make my mentor cannot be wrong. I am sorry."

"Well, you asked me what I want to tell you. Perhaps you want to know why I called you. I myself don't know why. Perhaps I did make a mistake after all. But now that I have called you back, I must say this: I am powerless to initiate you. Not only am I powerless, the task of initiating you is impossible for me. For me to initiate you, I might need to have you initiate me. And I am not ready for that." Kumargiri's eyes wandered to the moon nearing the horizon.

Chitralekha's face fell, and her eyes shone with kindness. She said softly, "Sir, your mistake saddens me more than it does you. What can I do? I cannot guess how your inability will shape my future, but I can say that you have already made a big impact on me. Till now, I had hoped that some time in the future you might ordain me, initiate me...but now that hope is lost. In your view, my life is shrouded in darkness; I want to see your light. My want cannot be fulfilled. I will blame my fate for that, I won't blame you!" Chitralekha stepped closer to Kumargiri.

The yogi stood still. Chitralekha reached out and held his hands. Kumargiri felt a strange shiver run through him—a shiver that brought him peace, joy. "Yes, perhaps it is impossible for us to be together. I am a woman, and you are a man. I am a dancer and you are yogi. I live in the realm of the senses and you live in the kingdom of spiritual seeking. These are competing forces. You came into my life like a dust storm, and you leave it like another one. It is all right. I will try not to meet you again. But before we part, yogi, I want to have the dust of your feet touch my head." She fell at Kumargiri's feet.

Kumargiri's heart was palpitating. He was shocked at this turn of events. He bent to lift Chitralekha up, and his hands brushed against her breasts. Chitralekha was ecstatic at the contact. The yogi did not share her feeling. He had touched her by mistake.

"Beautiful one, why do you touch my feet?" he asked.

Chitralekha stood united with Kumargiri and brought her face close to his. "You are my deity," she said.

Chitralekha's eyes sought out Kumargiri's. They worked their magic on him. Chitralekha brought her mouth closer to his. Kumargiri did not flinch. His breath turned warm and his whole body trembled.

"Master!" a voice called out to him.

He started and jerked back from Chitralekha like a man cautioned about a snake poised to bite him. It was Vishaldeva. Kumargiri burned with shame, and wished the earth would swallow him. He had been trampled by the dancer, in front of his disciple.

And Chitralekha was furious with Vishaldeva. He had no right to burst in on them. She hissed at him, "Young man! Who are you, and what brings you here?"

"I am the master's disciple, and I came looking for him when he did not return so late into the night," Vishaldeva said.

Chitralekha murmured to herself, "Such is my fate." She turned to Kumargiri and said, "Well, I shall leave now, master. Please do keep in mind that I want to be initiated by you, and you will have to initiate me." She spoke with a soft, serious tone that carried the gravity of a lady who was used to commanding others. "I want to come out of the noisy crowd and enter the sphere of peace. I want to forsake *maya* and partake of *brahma*. I am giving you time, master, so that you can think about this. You are higher than ordinary mortals, and you have nothing to fear from me. You have won over desire and passion, master, and I worship you. This servant salutes your feet." She walked away.

Kumargiri held Vishaldeva's hand tightly. "You are a fool," he said. The moon had sunk below the horizon.

Chapter Seven

hwetank!"

"Master?"

"Tell me what you saw today!"

"The mistress trounced yogi Kumargiri. I am so happy."

"You are happy!" Beejgupta snorted. "You are happy, but I am sorry. You will wonder why. You can laugh, and so do I, but my inner self weeps."

Shwetank was surprised. "Master, I do not understand you," he said.

"Ah Shwetank, you do not understand me...that's right, how could you? You have not seen the world; you are not experienced. What you consider Chitralekha's triumph is her utter defeat. Chitralekha and Kumargiri! Neither of them is a victor; both are losers. The wheel of fortune is spinning fast, and they are caught in it."

Shwetank was still perplexed. The chariot reached Beejgupta's mansion, and they alighted. Beejgupta held

Shwetank's hand. "I want to talk to you. Come along. Sit with me a while."

The master and the servant went into the study room. Beejgupta commanded Shwetank to sit, as he himself sat and said, "Shwetank, do you know why Kumargiri lost?"

"No!"

"Allow me to unravel the mystery. You do not know Chitralekha as much as I do. She has a superior and influential personality. Kumargiri is a wise yogi. He detests lustful passion, and Chitralekha—though she is wise—is against spiritual seeking. Kumargiri and Chitralekha are both full of ego and slaves to their feeling of mine-ness. But their means are exactly contrary—one has sought refuge in the spiritual path, and the other in self-confidence. What happened today has pushed them both away from these means that they had adopted. In the near future, they will lose their unique energies."

This still seemed a riddle to Shwetank. He said, "Master, your thought process is too deep for me."

"I neither have the capability to say these things in a clearer way, nor do I think it proper to do so," Beejgupta said. "If you do want to know, just do as I say."

"The master only has to say the word," Shwetank said.

Beejgupta said, "Go and congratulate her tonight, and study her expression when you do it."

Shwetank left immediately for Chitralekha's house. It was still lit. Inside, there was a crowd of young courtiers who had come to congratulate her. Her maids were welcoming visitors and serving them, but Chitralekha herself was nowhere to be seen. Shwetank asked one of the maids, "Where is the mistress?" She took Shwetank into a well-decorated inner room, and asked him to take a seat. "The mistress has not returned. She should be here any time," she said.

Shwetank started waiting. The crowd of disappointed courtiers started thinning. The hours passed, the last courtier left but Chitralekha did not come. Shwetank was surprised. Where might she be? He asked the maid again, "When is the mistress likely to return?" She said she could not say.

Shwetank's patience was wearing thin. It was almost midnight, and there was still no sign of Chitralekha. Shwetank was tempted to return home, but curiosity held him back. The mid-night bell rang. Shwetank stood up with a sigh. He said to the maid, "When the mistress returns, tell her that I had come to congratulate her." He walked out of her house, and saw Chitralekha's chariot in the distance, heading towards him. He stopped there.

The chariot drew near and stopped, and Shwetank helped Chitralekha alight. She smiled at him, and asked, "How are you? And what keeps you awake so late?"

Shwetank chuckled. "I came to congratulate you!" he said.

He held her hand as they walked to her dressing room. "Wait for me in the guest room, Shwetank. I will come soon."

In a short while, she had changed into a white sari and joined him. "Well Shwetank, you have come to congratulate me. What about?"

"On your victory."

"On my victory..." Chitralekha face, that had been radiant, turned pale. For the first time, Shwetank glimpsed a shade of sorrow hidden behind her layers of youthful ardour. He could not understand it. Every emotional change in a beautiful face has a beauty to it; the paleness and grief of Chitralekha's face, accentuated by the play of light from a hundred lamps, enthralled Shwetank. "On my victory," she repeated. "Shwetank, I am not worthy of congratulations. I did not win. It was a major defeat for me."

Chitralekha had spoken in Beejgupta's words! And both of them had spoken in grave tones. Shwetank was stunned.

Chitralekha read his face. "You are surprised, and there is no reason not to be surprised. Do you know where I have been?"

"That is what I wanted to ask," Shwetank said. "I did not dare to."

"I was in Kumargiri's hut. I had no reason, and no right, to insult him and make him feel small. My sphere is different, and I should not have trespassed into the sphere of wise men, whatever I think of their wisdom. What I did was evil. I had gone to ask him for forgiveness.

Shwetank was dumbfounded. What was all this? It was beyond him. He spoke: "But bringing out the truth is every one's right. It is our duty to expose those who deceive men, to show them for what they are. Lady, what you did was right!"

"That is precisely what I repent for. The whole world may think I was right, but I don't. Kumargiri

is a yogi and his has a positive energy. His Truth and
his God were both imaginary, but on the other hand
it is impossible for other men to attain his imaginative
power. What is the fountainhead of his imagination?
That is the question. Kumargiri has the energy to create. What I did was an act of destruction, of dissolution.
An individual's excellence is revealed in proving rather
than refuting, creating rather than spoiling."

"But if someone builds a house that harms those
who live in it, should we not destroy it?"

"It is no use arguing," Chitralekha said. "I feel that
what I did was wrong. But it is done. I must live with its
consequences."

"Consequences!" Shwetank's mind reeled from
this new angle. "What consequences, lady?"

"You will know soon enough," Chitralekha said as
she summoned a maid.

"I have not dined," she said. "And Shwetank, perhaps you have not, either?" She ordered the maid to
serve dinner for both of them.

After the maid left, Chitralekha brought out a
pitcher of wine. She drew a bowl for herself, and handed
Shwetank another bowl. Shwetank had become an
experienced drinker by then. He drained his bowl. Chitralekha said to him, "Shwetank, I am fond of you, and
one shouldn't hid things from those one is fond of."

Shwetank became even more her slave at these
words. "My lady, I assure that I am not lacking in empathy for you in any way."

Chitralekha reached out and held his hand. "Shwetank, promise me you will not tell my secret to anyone."

"I promise you, mistress!" Shwetank said.

"And you shall help me."

"Yes, I vow to."

"My victory today was hollow. It was my defeat. Kumargiri has made a huge impact on me."

Shwetank sensed the terrible truth that Beejgupta had hinted at. To repel his disbelief, he asked, "How?"

"You ask how? Do you not understand? I am in love with Kumargiri. I feel that he and I have a relationship that goes back many aeons. Today that yogi man defeated all the wise men of India, but not me. That happened because I know Kumargiri and he knows me. We were united in our earlier lives."

Shwetank believed in reincarnation—he did not question Chitralekha. "Yes, I understand."

"From the day I saw Kumargiri," Chitralekha continued, "I have been drawn to him. Only one who has gauged the depth of his soul can understand him. I know him well, and his inner self too. Shwetank! Kumargiri is the prime mover of my life!"

"I understand now, mistress. But how can I help you?" Shwetank said.

The maid brought their dinner and laid it in front of them. Chitralekha ordered Shwetank to eat, and started eating as well. They were silent.

After they had eaten, Chitralekha said, "You asked how you can help me. You can help me by not telling my secret to Beejgupta. He will have his doubts about me, but your job will be to dispel his doubts."

Shwetank thought about this. It was difficult for him to do Chitralekha's bidding. Beejgupta was his master. What Chitralekha had just asked him to do amounted to cheating his master. On the other hand, Chitralekha was his mistress. And then...

Chitralekha read his emotions. With a winning smile, she raised a bowl of wine to his lips. Shwetank gulped it down. Still smiling, Chitralekha asked him, "Tell me, will you help me?"

Shwetank was mum. He could not bring himself to say yes, or no.

Chitralekha's smile disappeared. Her flushed cheeks puckered as anger overtook her. Her delicate hands trembled. She grasped Shwetank's hand. "Shwetank, you must do as I say. That is an order."

Shwetank shrank back before her controlled fury. He mumbled, "As you say. I accept."

"You will have to take a vow before me!" Chitralekha said, and then paused for a moment. "No, there is no need for that. You have already given me your word, and I trust you will keep the sanctity of your promises in mind." With that, she raised a third bowl of wine to his lips.

Shwetank's eyes were closed. He savoured a rare pleasure. He drank the wine, and said, "My lady, I have always worshipped you. My life is intertwined with yours. You are my mistress, and I am your servant. I want you to believe that every sentence that you utter is like a sentence from the *vedas* for me. And as far as the sanctity of my promises is concerned, I can only say that I am not the kind of wretch who should be questioned on this count."

He stood up, and swayed a bit. "Will I have to arrange to have you escorted back today?" Chitralekha asked.

"No!" Shwetank was drunk, but he did not tremble, and he was in control of himself. "I am in my senses, and I will remain so." With that, he bowed and turned away.

When he returned home, Beejgupta's study room was still lit. A maid greeted him. "The master is waiting for you."

Shwetank entered the study room. Beejgupta was seated, deep in thought. Shwetank had never seen Beejgupta troubled. An empty wine bowl sat in front of him, and he looked like he was contemplating a bottomless sea of worry. It was as if a revolution had shaken up his kingdom of joy. He started, as if from sleep, when he saw Shwetank. "So you are back? It took very long."

Shwetank sat down. He poured cold water from an earthen pot into a bowl and guzzled it.

Beejgupta waited for a while, and then spoke again. "Shwetank, you have not answered me. What kept you so long?"

"Master, I was waiting for Chitralekha," Shwetank said.

"Did you say waiting for Chitralekha?" Beejgupta sat up erect. "You mean she was not at home when you got there?"

Shwetank hesitated. His promise was on his mind. "That's right, master. She was not at home."

Beejgupta saw the hesitation in Shwetank's words. He asked, "Perhaps she told you where she had been?"

Shwetank was torn by conflicting thoughts, but he did not have time to come to a clear decision. He spoke without faltering. "The mistress did not say anything, but it seems she was invited to Minister Chanakya's place."

Beejgupta felt an oppressive burden lift from his heart. He did not know how his heart had developed the notion that Chitralekha had gone to Kumargiri. Shwetank's answer reassured him. He asked Shwetank, "Well, did you congratulate her?"

"Yes!" Shwetank said. "But she said she did not deserve congratulations. She took no pride in her victory, not even satisfaction. I was surprised. She was saddened by the episode."

Beejgupta's eyes were moist. "What did I tell you?" he said. "Her rejection of the victory shows that she was defeated."

"I have only partly understood you, sir," Shwetank said.

"There is no such thing as partial understanding," Beejgupta said. "Either you understand something completely, or not at all." He stood up wearily, and continued, "Remember, Shwetank, man is a creature of independent thinking, but a slave of circumstances. And what is circumstance but a wheel that is turned by the karma of previous births. Man can triumph over circumstance only when he does not revolve with this wheel, but keeps a fixed eye on his duty. Chitralekha is trapped in the wheel of circumstances. Kumargiri's entry into her life is harmful to her, and so is her entry into his life harmful for him. Unfortunately, and without knowing, they will shatter each other's lifestyles. Only God can help them."

Chapter Eight

deep stillness settles on the calm ocean before a dreadful tempest. There is an electricity in the atmosphere as it senses the possibility of an upheaval. After that? There is nothing but the waves' dance of death, and the harsh, dissonant music of the storm.

Before a volcano erupts onto the bosom of the sky, there is a deep disquiet in the air. The blueness of the sky morphs into a dusty grey, and the air around the volcano empties out. And after that? A rain of fire.

Chitralekha's chariot stopped at Beejgupta's door. It was dusk after a hot day, and the roads teemed with the chariots of courtiers. Gardener women were peddling garlands of flowers to the ladies. Cool, fragrant glasses of drink kissed the lips of the courtiers and the ladies. Happiness was in the air.

The royal path was the centre of festivity. The girls flocked to the jewellers, and the young men to the tobacconists. Beejgupta was one of the crowd.

Shwetank was readying himself to step out. His chariot stood at the door, and a maid was helping him dress. A guard came in and said, "Master, the mistress' chariot is waiting at the door for you."

Shwetank was surprised. He was uncomfortable with Beejgupta's absence at this time. He had already sinned, and he suspected that he would have to commit more sins, for which he was not at all prepared. Still, he had no choice but to say, "Tell her I will be out very soon."

He stepped out, looking his usual well-groomed and handsome self. "What is your command, lady?" he asked Chitralekha.

Chitralekha looked into his eyes and smiled. She said, "I wanted to meet Beejgupta, but perhaps he is not at home?"

"The mistress is right," Shwetank said, fighting back a blush.

"Then I think I want to meet you."

"The lady obliges me. I am always ready to serve you."

"There is no need to be formal. I was a bit upset today, and I thought I would feel better if I spent the evening out with the crowds. I wanted to roam around—if Beejgupta isn't here, it's not a big problem. I have you."

"Very well," Shwetank said, and took a step towards his chariot. Chitralekha took his hand. "No—come with me," she said.

Shwetank sat in the chariot like someone under a spell. The chariot headed for the royal path. Shwetank held the reins while Chitralekha sat back. At the royal

path, Chitralekha asked for the reins. The horses recognised her touch, and they speeded up. They galloped
on to the royal path with their heads held high. Perhaps
they knew that the woman who held the reins could
make the most powerful of courtiers dance at her whim.
The rich and the powerful stopped for her chariot, and
people saluted and praised her. A few people taunted
Shwetank for sitting next to her, but Chitralekha
brushed them aside with her imperious presence.

In no time, Chitralekha was laden with flower garlands. Every one of the young men threw a garland at
her and she obliged them all by putting the garlands on.
Riding proud on her chariot, she resembled Shiva's con-
sort as she accepted the obeisance of the people who
bowed and showed their admiration for her. It seemed
as the whole throng on the royal path was there to welcome her.

Another chariot approached from the other side,
and stopped near hers. Chitralekha had stopped her
chariot and was engrossed in talking to a young man
in the crowd. As the other chariot stopped by, her attention flickered to it. The rider was none other than
Beejgupta—he was beaming with pleasure.

"It is a surprise to see Chitralekha here, on the
royal path," he said.

"And not finding Beejgupta at home surprised me,"
Chitralekha replied.

They both understood the undertones in their
banter. Shwetank stepped down from the chariot. "Chitralekha is cordially invited to Beejgupta's place. Perhaps
the invitation will not be refused?"

"Chitralekha happily accepts Beejgupta's invitation," came the answer.

Dusk had set in, and the street lamps on the royal path were lit up. Beejgupta dismounted and climbed on to Chitralekha's chariot. He took the reins. Shwetank took charge of Beejgupta's chariot.

Both chariots headed for Beejgupta's mansion. Beejgupta said, "I am sorry I wasn't there when you dropped by."

"No apology is due," Chitralekha said, smiling. "It is my fault—I came at an unusual time, so it was natural that you were not there."

Chitralekha was silent for a few moments, and so was Beejgupta. Beejgupta broke the pause. "Chitralekha! My mind has been uneasy for some days now. Why, I wonder? I do not know myself. May I ask why you have not come over before today? What kept you away?"

Chitralekha raised her head to look into his eyes. "What kept me away? I did not feel like coming."

Beejgupta had not expected this reply. He had surmised that Chitralekha would give a roundabout answer. Her clear and true words angered him. He was angry with himself, as well as with her. "So you did not feel like coming! And why is that? I have the right to know!"

Chitralekha looked closely at Beejgupta. His face had hardened and he exuded a tinge of arrogance. She felt herself flushing red, but she controlled herself, and said, "The right to know? What right do men have on others? I have never understood that. Still, if you insist, know that I have been upset these days; in my turmoil I have been oblivious of my own self."

They reached Beejgupta's mansion, and Shwetank helped them down. The three of them went into Beejgupta's pleasure room. Shwetank started to walk away but Beejgupta stopped him, saying, "Stop, Shwetank. There is no need for you to leave."

Chitralekha interjected, "No, Shwetank is not needed here."

"On the other hand, there is no harm if he stays on," Beejgupta said with a chuckle. "It may even help this young man get some more experience." Shwetank stopped, and Beejgupta signalled him to pour the wine.

Shwetank had become used to serving wine. He poured out drinks for the three of them, and sat at a respectful distance from the couple.

"Well, Chitralekha, you just said that you were in turmoil, and that you were lost because of it. It must be a strange turmoil."

"Do I infer that Beejgupta is compelling me to analyse my state of mind?" Chitralekha asked.

"Not really," Beejgupta said. "It's only a request, so that I can better understand this state of yours."

"Since Beejgupta requests it, he should know that the agitation was extraordinary, and so was the cause. And also that Chitralekha is unable to say more," she said.

Beejgupta looked at Shwetank. "Chitralekha is unable…" he said softly. "This is the first instance since we have been together that Chitralekha hides something from me. Chitralekha has had a change of heart, and Beejgupta has a faint inkling of this change."

The wine was warming them. Putting a second bowl to her lips, Chitralekha took a sip and said, "In this changing world, it is not unnatural for a thing to change."

Beejgupta was stunned. He had not expected this reply. "What? Everything must change? Then I take it that Chitralekha's love can change."

Chitralekha felt a pang of regret. She had blurted out what came to her mind, without thinking that it would lead to this loaded question. She tried to cover up now. "No, Beejgupta's guess is wrong. Chitralekha's love is a deep sea. It does not change easily. But yes, I do think, love changes, in keeping with nature's laws."

Beejgupta realised that there was a core of truth in what Chitralekha had said, however bitter it was. She had said the right thing, in the right context. Beejgupta sensed a distancing between them. An unknown energy was pulling them apart.

"Chitralekha, you are wrong—love is associated with the soul, the inner self, not with nature. Nature governs lust, which is related to the outer form. Lust aims at this body, that nature has made beautiful. Love involves the soul, not the body. Change is the constant in nature; not in the self. The bond of souls is immortal."

"That's a strange thing to say" Chitralekha said. "That which is born, will die. One who is immortal is not born. Where there is creation, there is destruction. The soul itself is immortal because it is unborn, but love is not unborn. When one falls in love, love is born. The relationship has a birth. It must come to an end some time. Love and lust are different, yes, but the difference is that lust is a madness that is momentary and gets spent, while love is deep and lasting. The bonding of souls is not immortal, Beejgupta."

Beejgupta saw that Chitralekha's argumentative power had increased manifold. His attack had missed the mark, and he felt a pain in his heart. "You may be right," he said. "I do not deny that. It's a matter of belief. But I do think the difference between lust and love is the same as that between craving and knowledge. Craving is unstable, and knowledge is stable—it is not erased, even if it disappears for a few moments. When madness is on the offensive, knowledge seems to retreat, but when the madness subsides knowledge occupies its stage again. If knowledge, *gyana*, is not immortal, then so is love not immortal. In my mind, *gyana* is immortal, along with God—and so is love."

Chitralekha was reclining by then, and her eyes were drowsy. Her beautiful face glowed with emotion. She sat up, and said, "You are right, I was deluded. I had forgotten myself. Forgive me." She put her hands around Beejgupta's neck.

Shwetank saw this and stood up. Beejgupta's eyes were shining. He said, "Shwetank, you may leave."

CHAPTER NINE

he noblest of Aryans, Mrityunjay, was a *kshatriya*—a warrior—by birth, but a *brahman*—a scholar—by nature. This venerable courtier's household reflected restraint and austerity, rather than the usual opulence. People compared him to Videha, Sita's father, a comparison he had earned. The whole city knew his name, and very few men had his stature and personality. He eschewed the crowd with its cacophony, and found solace in meditation and quiet.

This *kshatriya* was affluent and influential. He was counted among the prime courtiers of the capital, and he had a high rank in the royal court. People would bow their heads on hearing his name, and his presence evoked devotion. He was acclaimed as a man possessing the inner energy that comes from vast spiritual seeking.

Mrityunjay did not have a son; he only had a daughter named Yashodhara. Being the only child, she got all of Mrityunjay's love. The ageing Mrityunjay was in search of a groom for Yashodhara. At the age of eighteen, her youth was in full bloom, while Mrityunjay was at a stage when it was logical was a person like him to attain nirvana, or freedom from the worldly life. Her inheritance alone would sway any young man to seek the hand of Yashodhara, but she was beautiful as well, and her beauty was extraordinary. Her calm face had not lost its innocence, and her sweet peals of laughter were still more like a child's than those of a woman. Her eyes, big and beautiful like a doe's still showed a timidity, and her cheeks still flushed pink with shyness. Yashodhara's youth was joyful and calm. She was not tainted by vanity, affectation or shallowness.

As it happened, Mrityunjay saw Beejgupta one day and realised that here was a young unmarried man from a good family. Mrityunjay's well-wishers—and this tribe included those who aspired to have Yashodhara as their daughter-in-law—told Mrityunjay not once, but many times, about Beejgupta's relations with Chitralekha. But Mrityunjay had a brushed them aside: "Beejgupta has been in the age in life when one is carried away by obsession. His future lies wide open, ahead of him, his possibilities are immense, he is educated. For now, he is floating on the sea of experience."

Beejgupta had an invitation to a celebration of Yashodhara's birthday. Beejgupta had last seen Yashodhara when she was a mere child. He did not know Mrityunjay very well. He was surprised to see the invitation, and his surprise increased when he saw that he was invited along with Chitralekha.

Beejgupta said to Chitralekha, "It's strange...do you know the venerable Mrityunjay?"

"Yes," she replied.

"And possibly his daughter Yashodhara as well?"

Chitralekha thought for a while, and said, "Yes, I think I have seen her a couple of times."

"I have an invitation to a celebration of her birthday. I do not know Mrityunjay all that well, so this invitation puzzles me. And even more surprising, you are invited along with me."

"That means my going is inappropriate," Chitralekha said.

"No! You have been invited with me. That implies that society recognises our relationship as a virtuous one."

Chitralekha sighed. "Beejgupta," she said, "I am only used to visiting the functions of high families as a dancer. If I go as your companion, it is possible that the society ladies will insult me. I do not know what I will do if that happens."

Beejgupta gave her a confident grin. "Trust me, no one will insult you when you are with me." He called out to Shwetank.

Beejgupta and Chitralekha climbed on to Beejgupta's chariot, while Shwetank took the reins. They reached Mrityunjay's mansion at the fixed time.

"The great courtier Beejgupta's chariot is at the door!" the guard announced. Mrityunjay and Yashodhara were at the door almost immediately. They greeted the guests with warmth. The group crossed the

doorway and entered the dance-hall. Almost everyone who mattered in the city was there. They cheered
Beejgupta and Chitralekha's arrival. Beejgupta and
Shwetank stayed with Mrityunjay, while Yashodhara escorted Chitralekha to the group of women.

Chitralekha was surprised when she saw
Yashodhara. She had been conceited and confident
about her beauty; seeing Yashodhara humbled her in an
instant. Yashodhara showed her warmth and respect,
and showed her to a seat. She sat down next to her.
Some of the other women took offence at this partiality
to Chitralekha.

Yashodhara had been very impressed when, many
years ago, she first saw Chitralekha dance. Today her father had ordered her to be with Chitralekha, and it was
an order she was happy to obey.

A group of young women gathered around Chitralekha. Some of them launched indirect assaults, and
some taunted her in more straightforward ways, but
Chitralekha did not mind them. She understood her
position all too well. A leading courtier's wife said, "I
congratulate the dancer Chitralekha for entering our
society as an equal."

The biting comment was met with an even more
bitter reply: "On the strength of her beauty, she does not
need to be congratulated by haughty women."

The women in the group looked at each other,
shocked. The sharpness of the retort had created ripples that reached the men. Beejgupta walked over. He
was afraid that he had been wrong, that Chitralekha had
been insulted. "What is the matter?" he asked.

Chitralekha's face was an enraged red. She swallowed her anger and her expression became relaxed. "Nothing—we were joking," she said with a little laugh.

Yashodhara was charmed by this change of emotion. "Sister," she said, "you are very skilled in the ways of the world."

"Why do you think I am so influential?" Chitralekha laughed again.

Her peals of laughter drew the attention of the young men. They asked Beejgupta to sing. A *veena*, a lute, was summoned for Beejgupta and he sang the Raaga Bageeshwari even as he coaxed the *veena*. The hubbub of conversation died down as the crowd listened to him, mesmerised. After Beejgupta's song and the applause, Mrityunjay himself took the *veena* and asked Yashodhara to sing. She also sang in Raaga Bageeshwari. The audience found her song insipid, following Beejgupta's powerful performance.

Chitralekha sensed this. "I have a request for Yashodhara," she said. "Will she sing a song in Raaga Kalyan?"

Mrityunjay, and the others, turned to her. Mrityunjay did not understand why she made the request, but a request it was, and it came from an invited guest. He played the notes of the Kalyaan on the *veena*, and Yashodhara started singing. This time she cast a spell on the audience and the room rang with murmurs of appreciation. After she stopped, Chitralekha said, "Sister Yashodhara, I congratulate you for singing so beautifully."

Mrityunjay now understood why Chitralekha had made her request. She had the ability to gauge a singer's forte. "And Chitralekha," he said, "I thank you on Yashodhara's behalf."

Beejgupta bowed slightly and said, "May I now request Chitralekha to show us her dance?"

Chitralekha smiled. "Beejgupta's wish is my command."

This time Mrityunjay played the *veena*, and Beejgupta the *tabla*. Chitralekha started dancing, with her usual hypnotic effect on the people. Only a few minutes into her performance, the guard's cry rang out: "Yogi Kumargiri and his disciple are at the gate!"

Mrityunjay had to stop playing the veena and step out with an apology to receive Kumargiri. Chitralekha stopped dancing as soon as the veena stopped.

Mrityunjay brought Kumargiri and Vishaldeva in to the hall. The guests flocked to see Kumargiri. Chitralekha said to Beejgupta, "I will leave now. I have been insulted enough."

"How so?" Beejgupta asked.

"Art has the highest position, in my view. A man who insults art is an animal. How do I interpret Mrityunjay's stopping the dance to receive Kumargiri? Isn't it an insult?"

Beejgupta smiled. "As you wish."

Kumargiri had taken his seat. Chitralekha advanced to him and welcomed him. Then she turned to Mrityunjay and said, "I request your permission to leave."

Before Mrityunjay could answer, Kumargiri said, "Why, is my presence uninteresting? Well, perhaps that is natural?" His child-like laughter filled the hall like a melody.

Chitralekha replied carefully, "No, yogi, your presence cannot be uninteresting to anyone in this world. I have a different reason for leaving."

"But you did not choose the right moment to leave."

"Then I will not leave."

Mrityunjay took up the veena again, but Chitralekha signalled that she would not dance. This time Yashodhara stepped forward and said, "Sister, I did not refuse you, and now it is my turn to ask, and I know you will not refuse me."

Chitralekha did not refuse her. She took a deep breath, composed herself, and resumed her performance. Kumargiri looked at Yashodhara, and something about her held his attention. He compared the beauty of Chitralekha and Yashodhara. Both were supremely beautiful, but one had the kind of beauty that intoxicated, while the other's beauty had a calming effect. Chitralekha's dance was the splitting image of her liveliness, while Yashodhara's countenance was like a fathomless sea in which a man could lose himself. Kumargiri realised that he was being sucked into the sensual world. The liveliness of love was winning over the inactivity of asceticism.

Chitralekha's dance ended to a round of applause. Mrityunjay asked a maid, "How much time before dinner is ready?"

"It is ready. We are waiting for your order," the maid said.

The guests filed into the dining room and took their seats. The maids served them. Beejgupta, Yashodhara, Chitralekha and Shwetank sat next to each other. With dinner, conversation started as well. Beejgupta said, "Yashodhara, this is the first time we have interacted closely. I am delighted to meet you."

For the first time in her life, Yashodhara's lowered eyelids felt heavy and she could not raise them to look into a man's eyes. Her heart thudded, and had to make an effort to control herself. She replied softly, "There is nothing special about meeting me."

Chitralekha said, "God willing, this interaction will deepen into a deeper acquaintance that will grow into a relationship for life."

Yashodhara looked at her with gratitude; Beejgupta with alarm. Shwetank had eyes only for Yashodhara. Suddenly Yashodhara's gaze locked with his. Until then, she had not paid attention to him. In fact, she recognised everyone of the guests except for him. She turned to Beejgupta and asked him, "Who is this young man?"

"My servant—and younger brother!" Beejgupta said with a smile.

"Servant...and brother?" Yashodhara was curious. "How so?"

"It's like this: Shwetank here is a *kshatriya* from a high family, but he is a celibate bachelor who has lived with his guru. This guru, a renowned sage, sent him to me to learn the ways of the world; about sin in particular. He is entering society under my tutelage."

Yashodhara looked surprised. "His guru sent him to you to learn about sin! Is that really the right approach to show someone what sin is—for him to be associated with you?"

How innocent this girl was, how deluded, Beejgupta wondered to himself. He said, "Perhaps the biggest of sinners will not say that he is one. Each of us thinks he or she is good and virtuous. It hard to understand oneself. If Shwetank concludes that I am a sinner, I really am one."

Yashodhara was disheartened. The man to whom marriage had seemed pleasing a moment ago was chosen by a great guru to be the means for his disciple to learn about sin! She looked at Shwetank—he seemed innocent and handsome. And Beejgupta?

At the end of the meal, people washed their mouths and hands in bowls served to them. Beejgupta took Shwetank by hand and formally introduced him to Mrityunjay.

CHAPTER TEN

he lights still burned bright in Mrityunjay's mansion, but there was less life in it. The less important guests had departed, and the main actors remained. Mrityunjay had detained Kumargiri, Vishaldeva, Chitralekha, Beejgupta and Shwetank. After a long silence, Mrityunjay clasped Beejgupta's hand.

"Courtier Beejgupta," he said in a strained voice, "there was a secret motive behind today's gathering, and you have a lot to do with that secret." He looked at Yashodhara with a meaningful glance. Beejgupta's face fell, and Chitralekha's eyes twinkled. "I am hopeful that this elder's suggestion will not be refused," Mrityunjay continued.

Everyone had understood Mrityunjay, but Beejgupta stonewalled. "Sir, acceptance or refusal depends on the proposal," he said. "My answer will follow the appropriateness of your proposal."

Mrityunjay pondered this. "Beejgupta, you are not married?" he asked in a patient tone.

Beejgupta looked at Chitralekha. He fumbled for an answer. Mrityunjay was right, but also wrong. Beejgupta weighed his words: "Not according to the scriptures."

This time Kumargiri spoke in a grave tone. "Young man, can there be a marriage not in accordance with the scriptures?"

"The lasting relation between a man and a woman is marriage," Beejgupta said.

Kumargiri laughed. "But the very word 'marriage' is created by society. The scriptures sanctify the relationship between man and woman, and that gives the relationship society's approval. Beejgupta, you seek refuge in a half-truth!"

Beejgupta replied with the same seriousness. "King of yogis, there are no half-truths. This is no time to argue. I will reserve my answer." He turned to Mrityunjay. "Arya! I said that I am not married in the official sense. Let me make myself clear. I am unmarried in the eyes of society, but I am married to Chitralekha in reality. I have not married her in the way the scriptures prescribe, and I cannot do so in our society. But our relation is that of man and wife. I believe in love, and under these circumstances it is impossible for me to marry in the socially approved way, because no other woman can claim the right to my love." Beejgupta said this with his gaze lowered.

Mrityunjay spoke. "Beejgupta, you may be right. The fact remains that you are unmarried as long as

society deems it so. And as for love, I only have to re-
mind you that marriages are performed to get sons.
Chitralekha's offspring cannot be Beejgupta's heirs.
Have you thought about that?"

Beejgupta had, in fact, never considered this. He
did not have an answer. Mrityunjay then turned to Chitralekha. "Lady," he said. "You are wise. I will not waste
words explaining things to you. I am sure you understand Beejgupta's position."

Chitralekha had stayed quiet all this time. She
spoke up now. "Best of Aryans, you are completely
right. I am a social outcast, a dancer, and it is impossible
for me to be Beejgupta's wife. I am inclined to do what is
good for him. You do know, however, that it will mean a
great sacrifice on my part."

"A sacrifice?" Kumargiri interjected. "That's
strange. Perhaps you forget your natural inclination.
Remember, you once told me that you want to lead a
life of dispassion. This is the time to make that move."

Beejgupta was startled at this exchange. "Yogi Kumargiri," he said, "if you believe in dispassion and you
preach it, why are you pushing me into bondage?"

"Because dispassion is not for you. And you are
very much a social person. It is only right that you follow society's rules."

Chitralekha had been brooding. She said, "Yogi, I
will ask another question. Will you initiate me into a
spiritual life? If yes, then I will become your disciple
right now."

Kumargiri's gaze turned to Vishaldeva, who had
his eyes on him. Kumargiri thought for a long time

before replying. "Dancer Chitralekha, it is impossible for me to initiate you."

Chitralekha laughed. "It is easier to talk than to do. Yogi, dispassion is all very well for you, but it is very difficult for me. It is not possible for me to leave the world of passions on my own. I am in the sphere of love. The world does not see it as pious, but in my view and as the Almighty is my witness, it is. Leaving this sphere of comfort means entering a zone of pollution, and I am not ready to sin in vain."

Mrityunjay thought the matter was almost settled, but came undone.

Beejgupta thought the matter had almost come undone, but thankfully it stayed settled.

Kumargiri knew Chitralekha; she knew him. Shwetank and Vishaldeva understood the undercurrents. Yashodhara was clueless, ignorant and inexperienced. She said to Mrityunjay, "Father, it is late."

The old man looked at his daughter and then at Chitralekha. How different they were! One was an angel, the other a demoness. One was pure, the other was a seductress. Beejgupta himself, he thought, was an unfortunate victim of the wheel of fortune, but he was a humane person.

"Who calls your sphere impious?" he said to Chitralekha. "What you do is in keeping with your nature. And I do think that everything you do is for love. There is no room for impurity in love, lady, but is it not your duty to set the man you love on the right path, if he is astray? Love demands sacrifice, and if you do make the sacrifice I ask of you, it will be a great one."

His cogent words made an impact on Chitralekha, but Beejgupta interrupted. "Sir, it is no use saying this to Chitralekha. It is my duty to progress, or regress. Chitralekha cannot do it for me. And I can say from the bottom of my heart that my relationship with Chitralekha is immortal."

Beejgupta rose to his feet, but Chitralekha stayed seated. "Noblest of Aryans," she said to Beejgupta, "you may or may not be right. But I think I must set you free. Not for myself, but for Beejgupta. Trust me." Glancing towards Yashodhara, she addressed Mrityunjay: "And sir, Beejgupta will make your daughter a good husband. This will be a most beautiful wedding." Now she turned to Beejgupta. "Beejgupta, you will never find another wife like Yashodhara. From this moment on, you should treat her as your partner."

Beejgupta strode to the door. "Chitralekha, you are wrong to say that, and it is impossible for me to agree. I have nothing more to say." He turned to Mrityunjay. "Sir, I take your leave." With that, he left the mansion.

Chitralekha stood up hastily. "Sir, do not mind Beejgupta. Men forget the distinction between good and evil when they are excited. They should not be judged by what they say in the heat of the moment. I assure you that the union of Beejgupta and Yashodhara will be very favourable, and it is necessary." She bowed and followed Shwetank out of the mansion.

Mrityunjay took stock of the situation. After a pause, he said to Kumargiri, "King of yogis, I did not understand all of this, but I do understand very well that Chitralekha has a big influence on Beejgupta."

"You are right," Kumargiri said.

"And I also realised that in fact Chitralekha's heart is pure."

Kumargiri did not comment. His eyes strayed to Vishaldeva's. Vishaldeva betrayed no emotion, but smiled to himself.

Mrityunjay spoke again. "Is it proper to pressurise Beejgupta too much? That is the question. Chitralekha has spoken, and she will act on her words. But now I am inclined to think that I should leave Beejgupta alone, else I will hurt Chitralekha."

Kumargiri spoke up now. "I do not believe Chitralekha will be hurt. It is possible that Chitralekha is ready to leave Beejgupta. If that is so, Beejgupta's life will get a firm foundation. In my view, it is right for Beejgupta to separate from Chitralekha." He rose, and continued, "Mrityunjay, understand this—you will not find a better suitor than Beejgupta for Yashodhara."

CHAPTER ELEVEN

n her life, Chitralekha had defined love many times, and realised each time that she had been wrong—as wrong she was the last time.

Her first love was divine. She had loved her husband with a purity, an almost limitless devotion. She had more than immersed her personality in her husband's—she had erased her own self. She laughed to please him, spoke to please him and existed only for him. Each moment of her life was dedicated to him. Her husband was her love, her God and the reason for her existence. She had found happiness in this love. She had found the joy in submission that only those who submit in that manner know.

His death plunged her into darkness. She realised meditation and austerity did not help. She contemplated suicide, but she knew it was a great sin. She was told that austerity was an integral part of life, and that restraint was a widow's duty. Chitralekha tried this as well, but it turned out to be too hard for her. While her husband was alive, she could immerse herself in prayer and meditation—these activities had a basis, a firm foundation for her. In her widowhood, her single-mindedness and faith were shaken.

After that she loved Krishnaditya. This time it was not a divine love that possessed her—it was natural love. This love did not have the element of devotion; it was about immersion. She did not do away with her self. She formed a perfect union with her lover. For the first time, she felt the surge of lust, and it startled her.

She did not know the meaning of lust before that. She had obliterated herself in her love for her husband; she did not experience physical passion then. This time she did, and at first the wildness of her passion scared her. She felt a new energy stirring in her flesh. Love is not devotion, and therefore it cannot be one-sided. It is a relationship, and it must be mutual. It is a bond between souls. It is accompanied by vibrations, passion and mutual surrender. There is no place for satiation.

Krishnaditya left her. Chitralekha understood that love is not immortal. A pure memory can dwindle day by day till it vanishes.

Beejgupta entered her life. This time Chitralekha only felt passion, and, some times, self-oblivion—never self-sacrifice. She saw the intoxicating side of love. Together with love, she saw the beauty of opulence and indulgence. She learnt that life is not only about love, and love is not the only pillar of life. There are other expressions of life. Love itself can be the basis for a few days of happiness. Making this happiness last demands that one become oblivious of oneself, which is not natural. It takes wine to make that possible.

And then she was attracted to Kumargiri. He was young, handsome, intelligent and…She lost track of her thoughts. She was drawn to Kumargiri without willing it. She did understand that, but did she even understand her will?

This time, Chitralekha's love for Kumargiri blossomed in Beejgupta's presence. She was not brave enough to go to Kumargiri.

The function at Mrityunjay's mansion gave her the courage she needed, and a pretext to deceive Beejgupta's humaneness. She said to herself, "It is my duty to see Beejgupta at peace. Freeing him will mean a huge loss to me, but it will give him a path to progress. I will have to leave him to free him."

Chitralekha spent a sleepless night. Her mind reeled with these thoughts. It was only in the early morning that she sank into an exhausted sleep. She woke up late, at midday. She asked the maid if there was a message from Beejgupta. There wasn't.

She went for a bath, and refused to eat. She ordered her chariot to be readied, and went into her dressing room. Slowly, she removed the ornaments that had been her constant companions. She wore a sari in the holy colour of saffron. She did not tie her hair. She stepped out and saw that the chariot was at her door.

She wrote a letter to Beejgupta, and ordered a maid to get it delivered if she was not back by evening. She entrusted her household to another trusted maid, saying to her, "Don't be surprised, Sunaina! I am giving up this life of luxury for some time. Till I return, you are the mistress of this house."

She climbed on to the chariot and moved towards Kumargiri's hut. At the royal path, she told the charioteer to stop, and wait for her. If she did not return by the end of the afternoon, he was to take the chariot back without her.

When she reached Kumargiri's hut, she found him in deep meditation. Chitralekha sat in front of him. After a few hours, when Kumargiri awoke from his trance and opened his eyes, he saw her sitting still. Her eyes were closed, and she was lost in thought.

She only wore a single cloth. Till then, Kumargiri had seen her glamorous and bedecked form, the exciting and intoxicating splendour of her body. This time he saw a Chitralekha who was at peace, one who radiated with an inner energy. The glow, and her outer saffron shell had cloaked her longing. Kumargiri could not take his eyes off her wondrous form. He spoke softly. "Dancer!"

Chitralekha opened her eyes. "Is the mentor's trance ended?"

"Yes, but, dancer, what brings you here?"

"The desire for initiation."

"But I had refused to initiate you."

"Yes, but I still came. I have made a sacrifice. I have given up all my splendour, everything I had. All I am left with is the attachment to mine-ness. I have brought it to you. It is your duty, your dharma, to free me from it."

"No, dancer, no!" Kumargiri trembled before her wide eyes. "No, it is impossible! I cannot initiate you!" He lost his composure. "To ordain you means to fall. Fall very low! Where? To a bottomless pit! I know you, and I know myself! It is hard to uplift you...it is easy to lower myself."

Kumargiri got up. He stalked the hut like a distraught, trapped man. Chitralekha sat silent like a statue. Kumargiri stopped and turned to her. He said, "Dancer, tell the truth! I do not lie to you. I ask you to be true. Why did you come here? Do you really want to attain enlightenment? To give up pleasure? Is it possible? Speak now! Why are you quiet? You do not want to say the truth, and you cannot lie. Your silence tells me the answer."

Chitralekha woke up from her sleep-like state and looked into Kumargiri's eyes. She said calmly, "Yogi, remember once you had disregarded your victory and defeat, and told me the truth? I will be truthful to you. I have come to love you."

"Then my guess was not wrong! You have come to love me? Who never loved any one? Who does not know this kind of love? How strange! But let me ask one more thing. How does one love anybody? I used to think that love is born on its own. I did not know that one decides to love someone and then loves that person." Kumargiri laughed a dry, mirthless laugh.

Chitralekha recoiled. "Yogi, my words came out wrong. I love you. You know—you have known for a while. I have come to you so that you love me back. Now you know all there is to know."

"You love me—that is enough. I have never stopped you from loving me, and nor could I have stopped you if I had tried to. It may be right to expect love to be reciprocated, but it is wrong to try too hard to realise this expectation."

Chitralekha's face fell, but she guarded herself. She used a very grave tone. "You are right, yogi! I was wrong this time as well. I have come to quench my thirst. I have come here to faithfully serve at your feet, to drown myself in you. Service, faith, self-effacement, thirst—these make up love. I had sensed this truth, cloaked in trust and duty, when I was married; at that stage in my life the outer cloak hid the essential truth from me. Now I realise this truth. Here I am."

Now Kumargiri turned serious. "Is love possible without lust?" He asked himself. His training and his instinct shouted, "No!" His heart said, "Fool! Lust has no place in true love."

"Give me some time, lady," Kumargiri said. "It is a difficult problem."

Chitralekha gripped his feet. "Sage, there is not time any more. It is done. I have committed myself to this path, and I cannot retreat. I have come to live in this hut, not to go away."

Kumargiri avoided a direct answer this time. "Have you come here on foot?" he asked.

"No, on my chariot," Chitralekha said.

"Where is it?"

"I left it on the royal path. The driver must have returned home with it by now."

Kumargiri looked skywards. He thought, "God, what is this mystery? What is your will? Your will be done." He turned to Chitralekha, who was lying at his feet, and guided her to stand. "Very well, lady. I will initiate you. If God wills me to struggle against worldly passions, so be it."

He summoned Vishaldeva and told him to build a hut for Chitralekha. Vishaldeva could not hide his surprise. He understood what was happening all too well. He bowed to Chitralekha and said, "Revered lady, you are welcome." He cast a meaningful glance at Kumargiri.

Kumargiri knew what was on Vishaldeva's mind. "Young man, you are surprised, aren't you? You have seen my weakness once, and it is natural for you to feel surprised. But remember this: it is man's due to overcome his defects. Today, God has revealed a truth to me. The supreme aim of life is to conquer lust. That is why I will initiate Chitralekha."

Vishaldeva smiled. "The Guru is right, as always. Shall I prepare the hut tonight?"

Vishaldeva's smile, and his question aroused a lightning-like anger in Kumargiri. He drew himself ramrod straight, and said, trembling, "No! Don't build the hut. Chitralekha will stay in mine. Do you understand, Vishaldeva? You dare to mock me? Because of that one lapse? Remember who I am—your Guru. I am higher than you. I will show you how strong a true yogi can be."

Vishaldeva cowered before the enraged Kumargiri. He fell at Kumargiri's feet. "Pardon me, master," he said. "I will build the hut right away."

"No!" Kumargiri thundered. "There is no need for a hut!" He took a deep breath. Once, in the grip of a delusion, I scoffed at your mentor, the great Ratnambar. This is my punishment for that transgression. Your guru sent you here to study the nature of sin, didn't he? Now you will see sin, and you will see me triumph over it. It is time for my meditation. You may leave."

Vishaldeva went away, crestfallen. Kumargiri looked at Chitralekha. "Lady," he said, "what just happened is like a dream. I myself cannot believe it. But what had to happen has passed. I do feel I am playing with fire, and it scares me…"

A sweet smile lit Chitralekha's face. "Sir, do not fear me. You will not find me obstructing your prayer and meditation. I promise you that. I love you, and love means limitless sacrifice. I will find joy in that which gives you joy."

"May it be thus," Kumargiri said, and sat in his straw mat. "You will have to get a mat of *kush* grass. You can ask Vishaldeva for the grass. Now it is time for me to meditate." He closed his eyes.

CHAPTER TWELVE

eejgupta realised, with the benefit of hindsight, that he had been rude to Mrityunjay without reason. When Shwetank met him the next morning, Beejgupta said, "Shwetank, I think I was a bit insulting at Mrityunjay's dinner yesterday. But I can't quite put my finger on what it was that I said. You were there, and you will remember the discussion—can you help me?"

Shwetank thought for a while, and then said, "The master only spoke in appropriate terms. And as for rudeness, even I understand that the talk was so transparent that the venerable Mrityunjay may well have felt insulted. But why worry over it? The truth is the truth, and people can differ on matters of principle."

"You are wrong, Shwetank," Beejgupta said. "The truth is the truth, but it does not have to be unpleasant. Whatever it was, I could have said it in a more likeable way."

Beejgupta was not as concerned about an affront to Mrityunjay, as he was about having hurt Yashodhara's feelings. He recalled her image—an image of love, her eyes serene and her face glowing with the flush of shyness. He could not bring himself to love her. She did not have the stunning effect that Chitralekha had on him. He could not tell if she had a pure heart like Chitralekha's. In Chitralekha, he had a wife whom he had not married, and a dancer who loved him for who he was—she did not need his money. He recalled the night when he had first met her. There was no comparison between Chitralekha and Yashodhara. Chitralekha was a grand lady. He wondered why he was even thinking about Yashodhara.

"Shwetank," he said, "it is my duty to apologise to Mrityunjay for my harshness."

"As the master commands."

"But I don't want to go there. I will send a letter that you must take to Mrityunjay." He wanted to forget Yashodhara.

Beejgupta wrote out the letter and handed it to Shwetank. Shwetank carried it to Mrityunjay's mansion. He asked the guard if the master was in. The guard said that he was out on work, and that he could take the letter.

"No! I can only give the letter to him in person," Shwetank said. "Or to his daughter." This last line escape him involuntarily.

The guard showed him in, and sent for Yashodhara. She came into the hall shortly after, and Shwetank stood up to greet her.

She greeted him with a *namaste* and asked, "What brings you here today?"

"Courtier Beejgupta has sent a letter for your father. I have come here with the letter." Shwetank avoided calling Beejgupta his master.

"Father should be here any time, but perhaps it will be inconvenient for you to wait?" Yashodhara asked. Her eyes were clear and sparkling.

"Who would find it inconvenient to be in the presence of the most beautiful lady in Patliputra?" Shwetank blurted out.

Yashodhara was not used to this kind of talk, from someone whom she had only known for a few moments. She found the words sweet. Her naturally pink cheeks became a deeper red, and she lowered her eyes with a smile. Shwetank was a guest anyway, and had a claim to her hospitality.

"You must know Arya Beejgupta very well?" she asked.

"Yes! No one should object to his being counted among the best men in the world."

"And what do you think about dancer Chitralekha?"

"She is divine—a very superior lady. The man who has known her has known beauty and understood a man's duty towards it."

"Then my guess was right—your name is Shwetank." Yashodhara said.

"The lady's guess is right."

"Arya Shwetank, may I ask a question? Did your mentor really send you to courtier Beejgupta to learn about sin? Is Beejgupta a model sinner?"

Shwetank smiled. "The lady is right—my guru did send me to Beejgupta to learn about sin. And as for his being a sinner, I have to confess you put me in a dilemma. On the other hand, my classmate, who accompanied yogi Kumargiri yesterday, has been sent to the yogi with the same aim, to find out what sin is. You will probably be surprised to know that."

Surprise was, in fact, written large on Yashodhara's face.

"But you shouldn't be. It is not a given that the people we were sent to are sinners. It is very likely that those who are in contact with them will be sinners. Then there is also the basic question—what is sin? Who knows? What I consider sin may not appear as sinful to another person, and conversely, many things we do not even pay attention to may be sins to others.

Yashodhara was not satisfied with this explanation. "Arya Shwetank," she said, "I can say this much—you believe in seeing good qualities in people."

Mrityunjay stepped into the hall, and Shwetank rose to salute him. Yashodhara greeted him as well, and left the room after excusing herself.

Mrityunjay asked Shwetank to be seated, and said, "Are you Beejgupta's servant?"

"You are right. My master has sent you this letter." Shwetank handed over the letter, which he still carried.

Mrityunjay took the letter and read it. His face softened. "Tell courtier Beejgupta that there was no need for an apology. And my opinion about him remains as high as it was. Also, please tell him that if he is not too busy, he is welcome here in the evening, and for dinner." He paused for a moment. "Oh, and Shwetank, you are invited as well."

Shwetank beamed with pleasure. "Sir, your wish is our command. If the master comes, I will definitely be there. Of course, I cannot come without his permission."

Mrityunjay smiled, and said, "You are a well-behaved and dutiful young man. I am pleased to meet you. Which family are you from, what is your father's name, and where does he reside?"

"I am from the Suryavanshi family, my father's name is Vishvapati and he lives in the province of Kaushala," Shwetank said.

"So your father is Vishvapati and he lives in Kaushala. Did he study in Kashi?"

"That is right, Excellency."

"That is a coincidence indeed. Your father is my classmate. You are doubly welcome—you are like family to me."

Shwetank was delighted to hear about this connection. A hope sprang in his heart. Was marriage to Yashodhara possible? "Impossible!" his mind reasoned with him. His father's wealth was lost, and he now lived a simple village life. He was from a high family, but what of that? Mrityunjay was wealthier, more reputed and more powerful than his father. Marriage requires parity in such matters. However, the hope that had sprouted refused to wither away.

Seeing him quiet, Mrityunjay said, "Young man, consider this house as yours. I am surprised that Vishvapati did not tell me about your presence here."

"My father lives the life of a recluse. That is the most likely reason. I will take your leave, Excellency," Shwetank said.

It was time for lunch. "I trust you will not decline to join us for lunch?" Mrityunjay asked.

"There is no desire to decline, Sir, but I am Beejgupta's servant at this point in time. I cannot act without his orders. Do allow me to leave. It is quite late, and Arya Beejgupta will be waiting for me."

"Well said! You may leave, of course. And please do not forget to tell Beejgupta about my invitation."

Shwetank returned and conveyed the invitation to Beejgupta. "I am invited—but should I go?" Beejgupta pondered aloud. He thought about it all afternoon. He had a niggling feeling that it was not right for him to go, but he could not explain his reluctance to himself. After a long internal debate, he finally decided to go. A vague desire to see Yashodhara again, and to talk to her, had formed in his mind. To Shwetank, he only said, "I do not think we should turn down an invitation from a gentleman."

Thus it was that Beejgupta and Shwetank returned to Mrityunjay's mansion. This time there was peace, instead of the hustle and bustle of the last night. Mrityunjay welcomed them, and led them to the drawing room. Yashodhara was waiting for them.

"Arya Beejgupta, your letter was unnecessary," Mrityunjay said.

"Noblest of Aryans, it is a man's duty to acknowledge his lapses," Beejgupta replied.

Mrityunjay changed the topic with a laugh. "Your servant Shwetank is my classmate Vishvapati's son, and I only got to know about it today." He looked at Shwetank fondly.

"But sir, Shwetank is not my servant. He is a fellow disciple," Beejgupta said.

Mrityunjay nodded in approval. "You are a bit late today—did work hold you?"

"Yes, I have visitors from Kashi," Beejgupta said.

"I have heard that Kashi is a beautiful and ancient city," Yashodhara said. "Have you been there?"

"Oh yes, I have," Beejgupta said. "Some of the best years of my life were spent in Kashi. My guru, the great Ratnambar, lived there. Lady Yashodhara, Kashi is actually quite close by. I have in fact travelled much further—I have seen every corner of the north of India."

"Even the Himalayas?"

"Yes, I have even been to the Hindukush mountains in the west. Mountains are where we get to see the essential beauty of nature." He turned to Mrityunjay. "Excellency, I saw many amazing things in my journeys, but there is one incident I will never forget."

"Tell us about it!" Yashodhara said.

"Certainly," Beejgupta said. "About ten years back, when I was still a student, I went on a journey with Guru Ratnambar. We reached the city of Haridwar, after a long trek past big cities and forests along the River Ganga. The plains ended at Haridwar, and we were confronted by mountain peaks that reached for the skies. I asked the master what lay ahead, and he replied simply that it was unknown territory.

"A man sat on the river bank, and he had overheard us. 'Unknown territory? You may be right, but let me tell you: this land that lies ahead is the home of the Gods. These mountain ranges host Shiva's abode, Kailasha. It is land where the magical *gandharvas* dance and the celestial *apsaras* frolic.' A smile of disbelief flickered on Guru Ratnambar's face, but in my inexperienced youth, I was not capable of disbelief.

"'Great guru, can we cross these mountains and reach the lands of the Gods?' I asked.

"'Yes. If you want to go, I am with you,' the Guru said.

"We advanced into the mountains. We could not have imagined the pristine, rugged nature we encountered. The mountain breeze played with flowers of brilliant hues. The birds sang in melodies that our ears were not accustomed to, but still enjoyed. We had entered the kingdom of peace. We left the commotion and the crowds of civilisation behind us, and crossed mountain ranges each higher than the other. In the hamlets on the way, we saw fair locals. The women were beautiful; they wore multi-coloured clothes, and were fond of song and dance. They were not shy. I was a young man, and I was charmed by their beauty. They would file past in groups, singing as they went. I could not understand their songs, but I could guess that they were poetic, and that they were about love. I thought we had entered the land of nymphs.

"We kept going. The hamlets were smaller and at greater distances. The cold became more biting, and flowers and fruits less visible. One morning, we saw a mountain of gold. 'Gurudeva! We have reached Midas' mountain!' The great mentor laughed. 'We have reached the Himalayas. The sunshine on the snow looks like gold.' I felt embarrassed at my foolishness. We climbed higher. Now the earth was covered with patches of ice. We shivered with cold.

"The guru said, 'Let us turn back.'

"'No, great guru—let us keep going till that mountain, the one that is completely covered with snow,' I said.

"We went on and reached a small hut. Inside, we saw a woman sitting alone, thinking to herself. She saw us and rose. 'Welcome, guests,' she said with a smile.

"I noticed that the great Ratnambar looked at the woman very attentively. He then whispered to me, 'This place is not safe. Let us go back.'

"The woman cackled harshly. 'The wise old man guesses right. But now that you are here, you may as well keep going, so that you get to know one thing that you will remember for the rest of your lives.' The guru was chagrined, but it seemed as if he did not think it proper to argue.

"A little ahead, we saw a yogi seated on a hillock of ice. His matted hair reached his feet, and his nails looked like a lion's claws. He stared unblinking at us as we walked towards him. When we greeted him, he blessed us and signalled for us to sit by his side.

"'It is good to see you. It's ages since I last saw men,' he said with a sigh. His face was lined with grief.

"'Sir, you appear sad,' Guru Ratnambar said.

"'Yes, I am both sad and happy,' he replied, and he gestured towards his back. We stood and looked there, and the sight gave us goosebumps. We saw a blood-red pool with stairs leading into it. Only then did we notice the stench that came from it.

"The guru asked the yogi, 'Why do you not leave this place?'

"'I want to,' he replied, 'but I can't. I have lost track of the number of times I tried to leave. It's no use, there is no getting away!'

"After this we talked of spiritual matters. The stranger put forward his views on esoteric aspects of meditation and penance. We realised that he was highly knowledgeable. We bore the foul stench for hours just to listen to him talk. Darkness was falling. In the middle a sentence, the yogi abruptly got up and shouted, 'It is time!' He ran to the pond, and we followed him out of curiosity. He thrashed about like a man possessed, and then jumped into the water. At that very moment, the pool of foul blood turned into a lotus pond with inviting, clear water. Our jaws dropped! A woman joined the yogi in the pool, and we discerned that she was the one we had met in the hut earlier in the day. They started frolicking in the water. The woman laughed and said, 'Fools! Don't just stand there! Come, join in and enjoy yourselves.' I felt myself overcome by a desire to immerse myself in the water, and I started to undress. But the great guru Ratnambar held my wrist in an iron grip.

I don't know where he summoned the power from, but I just could not free my hand. The next thing I knew was that he was half dragging me away from there. As we passed the hut, panting, the guru said, 'Young man, thank the Almighty that we got away.'

"The image of that woman haunted me for many years."

"Did guru Ratnambar tell you the real story?" Yashodhara asked.

"No! In fact, he just said that there are many things in this world that are beyond comprehension, and that episode was one of them," Beejgupta said.

A little later, they proceeded to the dining hall. This time Beejgupta and Shwetank sat on either side of Yashodhara. The story was still on Yashodhara's mind. "Sir, your story is unique. I suspect I will never forget it. I really would like to experience strange things like that."

Beejgupta sighed. "Lady," he said with a smile, "we don't gain experiences—circumstances make us experienced."

Shwetank was looking for a chance to talk to Yashodhara. He said, "Lady, an entire lifetime of experiences stretches before you."

Yashodhara's expression became hard to decipher. "Perhaps," she said. "But every moment of this life is valuable. Isn't it a pity that some moments are wasted?"

Beejgupta laughed this time. "Well, there is an invisible hand behind every action of ours. There are two opposing camps of world view these days. One makes life full of action, the other makes life a centre of peace.

Both have attractive arguments. It is hard to make a choice!"

Shwetank realised that he could never impress Yashodhara with his personality in Beejgupta's presence. Still, he tried one more time. "Lady, we humans want to lead contented and happy lives, but we feel the pressure for activity. Love is our predetermined goal. The stirring of the heart, and the joy this stirring brings—these mark the sphere of love. Life is primarily about love. You see, it is essential to know other souls, and love is a deep empathy between two souls. It is life's most beautiful goal."

Yashodhara looked at Shwetank in a different way. The meeting of their eyes gave Shwetank goosebumps. The few moments of the glance were enough to make Shwetank feel drunk.

"This is life," Beejgupta said softly.

Yashodhara looked away jerkily and her face burned with guilt. Shwetank felt flustered, and he lowered his eyes.

CHAPTER THIRTEEN

ashodhara was attractive—she had an aura of sweet charm, but Beejgupta sensed a liveliness missing from it. In her, he felt, a man could see purity, imbibe it and become pure. He would not find joy. He had not known a persona like hers. Her impenetrable gravity seemed a riddle to him. Her clear, unpoetic style of talking had an austerity to it that he could respect, but not adopt.

Youth wants bustle. At every step, it seeks difficulties and embraces them. It treasures individuality. And it looks up to people with a clear, effective vision. The fusion of its energies with those of others can create a revolution, but by themselves, these energies are not as formidable.

Thus it was that Beejgupta had mixed feelings for Yashodhara. She was an image that would be worshipped in the temple of his heart. She had a blessed, idealistic feminism. She was a pillar of faith. Her eyes were calm and steadfast. And Beejgupta wanted a pulsating life, the surge of hot blood in his veins; he wanted to feel stirred. He did not want Yashodhara in his life.

One who has tasted wine, and known its intoxication, cannot live without it. Beejgupta could not leave Chitralekha.

When Beejgupta reached home after the dinner, a letter waited for him. It was a small, plain letter. And it contained a lifetime of experience, and a tome of philosophy. It went thus:

My love, my master,

Today I set out to do what I never expected to. I loved you. I still do. Love demands sacrifice, and I sacrifice myself. I have made your life meaningless. My love made an able man such as yourself ignore his duty. I must make amends for this. I thought it proper to abandon joy and embrace self-control—and that is why I am taking initiation from yogi Kumargiri. You must marry, if not for yourself, then at my request. You will never marry while I am there. I know that, and that is why I must part from you. As for me, I was a widow, love made me stray from my duty. I shall revert to the right path, the widow's life of abstinence.

Your Chitralekha

Beejgupta read the letter. His hands trembled, and his face turned pale. His heart thudded. He handed the

letter to Shwetank, and rushed to the bedroom, cover-
ing his face with his hands.

His fears had come true. Chitralekha and Kumargiri! What a pair! "It is impossible for them to stay
together for long!" he said to himself.

But what of that? How did it matter whether it was
possible or not? He had to face the question: why was
Chitralekha attracted to Kumargiri?

Was this love? Was even the relationship of souls
not immortal? Was Chitralekha right when she had told
him emphatically that love was not forever?

But was it even certain that Chitralekha had
stopped loving him? That was not what the letter said.
It spoke a different story: Chitralekha had adopted the
highest ideal of love by sacrificing herself. She had left
him to make him happy. Beejgupta cursed himself for
doubting Chitralekha. She was a goddess. But she had
erred—she had erred terribly. She may have wanted
to gift him happiness, but she had saddened him beyond measure. Beejgupta could not marry. Chitralekha
was the love of his life, and love and marriage are thick
relations.

Beejgupta could not sleep that night. He stopped
tossing around and got up. It was past midnight. He
stepped out of his mansion, and started walking towards Kumargiri's hut. His feet propelled him in that
direction.

Kumargiri's hut was lit when he reached it many
hours later. Kumargiri sat rigid on his mat, absorbed
in meditation. Chitralekha slept in a corner, on a mattress of *kush* grass. Except in their private moments,

Beejgupta had only seen Chitralekha in her glamorous form. He had never imagined he would see her without her ornaments, without her saffron paste, lying in the shadow of peace with the hint of a smile on her face. It seemed as if in her dream she was lying at the feet of the Goddess of peace. He gazed at her.

Morning was breaking. Kumargiri came out of his trance, and Chitralekha out of her sleep. Both saw Beejgupta, Kumargiri with clear eyes and Chitralekha with bleary eyes. "You? Beejgupta?" they said together, but not in concert.

Kumargiri was surprised. Chitralekha was afraid.

Beejgupta greeted Kumargiri first, then Chitralekha. Kumargiri blessed him. Chitralekha closed her eyes. Beejgupta called her gently, "Chitralekha!"

"Beejgupta!" she said.

Beejgupta had a lot to say, but words failed him. He took a deep breath and said, "Have you decided?"

Chitralekha bowed her head like a criminal. Two tear drops streaked her cheeks. "Beejgupta," she said in a broken voice, "what you see is my final decision."

"But you do have the right to think it over. Shouldn't you have asked me before taking a decision in the first place? Was I so separated from your life that you did not even feel the need to unburden your heart to me? Love does not distinguish between lovers. True love is a merger of souls. If you think that your walking away will compel me to marry, you are wrong. Don't imagine that you are making me happy with all this. In my life, I have only loved you, and I cannot love another woman. Marriage is not possible for me."

Chitralekha fell at his feet. For a moment, she was tempted to get up, take his hand, and walk away with him. But something stopped her. She was committed to another path, and there was no going back now. Sobs wracked her body. Beejgupta stooped and helped her up.

She controlled herself and said, "Beejgupta, you are an honourable person, more divine than human. I know you, but I also know that our love has made your life meaningless. You must marry. You say you love me—it is your duty to give me happiness. I will not find peace till I see you married, and your children treat me like a second mother. Remember that I will always love you, but do not let that get in the way of your marriage. Is pleasure the main part of love? Is love impossible without pleasure? I am only breaking our carnal bond—our spiritual bond will become stronger, you will see.

"Think again, Chitralekha. What you ask me to do is impossible," Beejgupta said.

Chitralekha put her arms around his neck and gazed into his eyes. "Beejgupta, let us part ways for some days. Perhaps you will change your mind? In any case, isn't there separation in love? Let us bear with our lovelorn state for a short time."

Beejgupta gently stepped away and looked out of the tiny window. His face, lit by the dim light, was impassive. "I have said what I had to. It is up to you to accept it. Let's do as you say, but I am sure that in little time you will realise you were wrong." He greeted both of them, and stepped out of the hut.

Chitralekha went with him to the royal path. There, they stopped and she gave him a lingering kiss. As they united, Beejgupta felt a burning passion in her kiss, a deep desire that he had not felt for years. Their eyes were misty when they separated. Chitralekha touched his feet, and murmured, "Beejgupta, it is possible that I am wrong. Forgive me for that!"

After the farewell, Chitralekha returned to the hut. Kumargiri was deep in thought. He signalled to her to sit on her mattress. "Chitralekha! You told me that you loved me. Was that true?" he asked.

Chitralekha was taken aback. "Yes, but what of that?"

"And yet you just told Beejgupta that you love him, and will keep loving him!" Kumargiri said.

"Yes, that is correct," Chitralekha said.

"But is it possible to love two men together?" Kumargiri's face was composed, but it had a shadow of disbelief.

"Do you think it is impossible?" Chitralekha replied. "Gurudeva, a man can have two wives and love both. Why can't a woman love two men? In any case, a woman can love her husband as much as her son. Relationships of the soul can be simultaneous."

"Chitralekha, you deceive me, or Beejgupta—or yourself," Kumargiri said.

"I do not deceive you, Gurudeva," Chitralekha said. "Trust me. I may deceive Beejgupta or myself."

"No Chitralekha! Think it over again. If you stay with me, you cannot love Beejgupta. Take that as a given. You must rise above the world. This is the place for dry austerity. There is no place here for the weakness of the heart. I grant you time to think deeply, and think again."

"I have thought it through, Gurudeva, and thought deeply. I will do as you say. I am even prepared to give up my attachment to myself—it is easier to give up the world."

Kumargiri was flummoxed by Chitralekha. She had a towering and influential personality, he reflected. His heart told him again that he should stop this talk of initiating her. He searched for an excuse. He said, "Lady Chitralekha, I am incapable of understanding you. Your individuality is not inferior to mine. I do not understand how I will initiate a lady such as yourself. I will have to understand this before I come to a decision. Until I can decide..."

Vishaldeva entered the hut before Kumargiri had completed his sentence. He bent and touched Kumargiri's feet, greeted Chitralekha, and went away for his morning duties.

Kumargiri waited till he had left. Then he took a deep breath and said, "What can I say. It seems God wants me to keep you here and test myself, and to give you the initiation you ask for. Dancer, forget what I just said."

Chapter Fourteen

ight follows day, day follows night. Sorrow follows joy, joy follows sorrow. Day does not have meaning without night, and joy has no value without sorrow. This is the iron law of change. Change is constant in the world, and man is part of this world.

Beejgupta had seen joy—it was inevitable that he would know sorrow. But Beejgupta was shaken by the sheer burden of his sorrow. He had not imagined the turn of events. He wondered what he was living for. Life became oppressive.

Still, bearing joy and sorrow is an integral part of the human design. It is cowardice to turn away from either of them. Beejgupta realised this, and he made up his mind to face the sorrow of separation from Chitralekha with courage.

There was one problem, though. As long as he lived in Patliputra, Chitralekha was within reach. What was the point in this proximate separation? And then there was a bigger question. When the other courtiers found out that Chitralekha had left Beejgupta so that she could immerse herself in spiritual matters, how would he save face? And finally, there was this third question: could Yashodhara inspire his love?

Beejgupta spent an afternoon pondering the vexed situation he found himself in. The more he exercised his mind to break out of the web of problems, the more he found himself entangled in it. His heart ached and he felt exhausted.

It was evening. Shwetank had joined him. "I have an idea," Beejgupta said.

"What is it, sir?"

"Let us go to Kashi. I feel like being a tourist for a few days."

"So soon?" Shwetank asked, surprised. He wanted to act on his growing love for Yashodhara, and he was reluctant to leave the city. "Perhaps we could wait for a week or so? We will need time to arrange things."

"No, we will leave the day after tomorrow," Beejgupta said in a dry voice which brooked no dissent. "The arrangements should take a few moments. You will just have to make preparations for the two of us."

"As the master commands."

Shwetank spent a sleepless night. He did not like Beejgupta's decision, but there was nothing he could do about it. He dared not refuse to accompany Beejgupta—that would be wretched behaviour. In the morning, he asked for permission to meet Mrityunjay before leaving.

"Why do you want to go there?" Beejgupta asked, though he knew the answer.

"I will be out with you, sir, and we will probably be gone for many days. I thought I should bid him farewell."

"You may go," Beejgupta said. He kept his smile to himself. Such was life, he thought. While he repented falling in love, here was Shwetank rushing in to love.

Mrityunjay was out working. Yashodhara met him in the drawing room. They greeted each other, and sat down.

Shwetank broke the silence. "Lady, I am leaving Patliputra with Beejgupta tomorrow. I have come today to bid you and your father farewell. It is possible that we will be out for many days."

Shwetank watched Yashodhara carefully, but she showed no trace of emotion. "I see," she said. "But even yesterday Beejgupta did not tell us about any such plans."

Shwetank was stung by Yashodhara's indifference. He spoke bluntly. "Yes, lady, he did not. Much has changed today. Yesterday Chitralekha left Beejgupta. She has gone to take initiation from yogi Kumargiri!"

He saw that Yashodhara was shaken. "What? Chitralekha has become a nun? Well, I can believe that Arya Beejgupta must have been saddened." She mulled the news for some more time, and then said, "I knew as soon as I met Chitralekha that she is a noble lady who would go to any lengths for Beejgupta's sake."

Shwetank felt defeated by the turn of discussion. His anger flared up now. "Arya Beejgupta can love no woman except Chitralekha. That is why he wants to leave the city. He needs a change of heart. I know him. His sorrow is so intense that if he stays in this atmosphere, he might commit suicide."

Now Yashodhara's face turned pale. "Shwetank, you are right," she said. "I do understand Arya Beejgupta a bit, and I see what you mean. We can't blame such a superior man as Arya Beejgupta for the state he is in. In fact, his reaction enhances my faith in him."

Shwetank was livid with anger by now. "Yashodhara," he said, "Is it really appropriate for Arya Beejgupta, or any other man, to be so crazed after a dancer? I do not know. And then, isn't it a sign of weakness to be so impulsive in sorrow?"

Yashodhara could not understand this sudden, unprovoked anger. She spoke in a serious tone. "Arya Shwetank, you may be right. I will not argue with you. But I still empathise with Beejgupta. Lady Chitralekha was not a dancer in Arya Beejgupta's view, she was like a wife. I know that, you know it, the whole world knows it. And we all have our weaknesses. No one is perfect. If we only befriend people without weaknesses, we will not have friends and life will become a burden. We may as well have a little sympathy for weaknesses."

Shwetank's frustration clouded his usually strong reasoning. "Sympathy and pity have nothing to do with duty. It is far better to criticise defects and help others remove them."

Yashodhara laughed. She was surprised at Shwetank's reactions, but she was enjoying the talk. "I guess we should first try to remove our own defects. Arya Shwetank, it is easy to list others' defects. It is common to refuse to acknowledge our own weaknesses. The better man is one who looks inward first."

Yashodhara's words pierced Shwetank's heart. He wondered if they were barbs aimed at him. Of course, they could also be innocuous words that just stated things as they were. He lowered his eyes, and said with a quiver in his voice, "I should not have criticised Arya Beejgupta in your presence. I am sorry. And yes, I will try to correct my own flaws first before pointing at others."

"In my presence?" Yashodhara said. Now she had reddened with anger. But in a moment, she realised why Shwetank had flared up, and she gulped. "Arya Shwetank, you are mistaken," she said. "I think I should tell you that I do not love Arya Beejgupta." Tears welled up in her eyes, and she hid her face in the folds of her sari.

Shwetank had blurted out his mind without any control, and he wished he could swallow his words. He folded his hands in a *namaste*, and said, "Lady, forgive me. I was beside myself. You probably don't know why I became so bitter."

"Why?" Yashodhara had guessed why, but she wanted to hear it from Shwetank.

"Because I love you."

Yashodhara's eyes met Shwetank's without any hesitation. "Now that is very surprising, Arya Shwetank."

Shwetank turned pale. What a terrible truth there was in that one line. Yashodhara did not love him. He said, "I know you do not love me, but I still love you. I would not have said it to you, because we are supposed to feel love and not go about stating it, but what could I do. Our discussion led me to the declaration. I am sorry. I should not have been so bitter to start with, and then so fearless."

"No apology is due, Arya Shwetank," Yashodhara said as she stood up. "I do not blame you. These things happen, and you can't be asking forgiveness every time. I will take your leave—let me see if father is back."

Yashodhara went away, and Shwetank got the feeling that he had made a huge mistake. He had come to meet Yashodhara, and luckily he was able to talk to her alone. He could have talked longer, much longer, if he had not angered her with his foolishness. How stupid he had been! He had sabotaged his own mission. He rose and stepped towards the main door, but Mrityunjay and Yashodhara entered the hall at that very moment. He greeted Mrityunjay.

"Please sit down, Shwetank," Mrityunjay said. "I am told you are setting out to travel the country with Arya Beejgupta. Is that correct?"

"Yes, noblest of Aryans," Shwetank said. "We leave tomorrow."

"And where do you plan to go?"

"To Kashi, sir."

"When do you plan to return?"

"I cannot say, sir. It is entirely up to Arya Beejgupta."

"Father, why do you never travel as a tourist?" Yashodhara asked. "I have never been to Kashi. Why don't we join Arya Beejgupta?"

The idea was not bad, Mrityunjay thought. Kashi was not too distant from Patliputra. He asked, "Daughter, how will we manage it with such little time?"

"Everything is possible, father," Yashodhara said. If you say the word, we can be ready to leave by evening."

Mrityunjay broke into a broad grin. "Yashodhara, this is the first time I have seen you being a bit stubborn. I cannot refuse you. If you can make arrangements, do so. Just one thing, you must handle it; do not trouble me."

Shwetank became even more despondent. Surely Yashodhara loved Beejgupta, and that was what was behind her keenness to go to Kashi. He consoled himself by thinking that at least Beejgupta did not love Yashodhara, and their time together would help Yashodhara to see who loved her.

Yashodhara said to him, "Arya Shwetank, so we will come with you. Do remember that, and please tell Arya Beejgupta."

"Why don't you make our travel arrangements first, Yashodhara?" Mrityunjay said. "If you do not finish on time, we will unnecessarily delay Beejgupta."

"I not finish on time? Don't even think about it." Yashodhara said. "Arya Shwetank, we will join you."

Shwetank rose with folded hands. "I will take your leave now. Sir, I will convey the message to Arya Beejgupta," he said. Then he turned to Yashodhara. "Lady, if you need help with the arrangements, I am available. I can come back in the evening."

Yashodhara smiled. "Thank you, Arya. When you come back in the evening, if there is work left to do, I will accept your help."

When Shwetank reached Beejgupta's mansion, he gave Beejgupta the news. Beejgupta was not at all happy to hear it. He had his reasons for fleeing Patliputra, and now one of the reasons was accompanying him. But he did not see a diplomatic way to refuse Mrityunjay. "Very well," he said in a disinterested way.

CHAPTER FIFTEEN

ashodhara kept her word, and they all departed for Kashi the next day.

It was night time. Nights are pleasant in summer, but that night held no pleasure for Beejgupta. A romantic full moon glowed on the eastern horizon; Beejgupta only sensed his heartache. Two rows of servants carried fire torches on either side. Beejgupta saw images of the embers that stung his heart within the sparks of the torches. He was quiet. Shwetank was with him on his chariot, while Yashodhara was with Mrityunjay on the other chariot.

The hours passed. It was after midnight. The silvery moonlight and the soft fragrance of jasmine bathed the land. Shwetank broke the silence: "Should we not stop for the night?"

Beejgupta was lost in thought. He would have been hard pressed to say what he was thinking. Thoughts of all kinds pummelled him, and he had lost track of time

in his agitated state. He was awakened from his reverie
not by Shwetank's question, but by the sound of Mrityunjay's chariot drawing near. Yashodhara called out over
the din of the chariots, "Arya Beejgupta, isn't it time to
break for the night?"

Beejgupta started. He looked up at the sky. The
moon had traversed the sky towards the west. He turned
to Shwetank and said, "Shwetank, give orders to stop,
and see if you can find a garden near by for a halt."

The procession ground to a halt, and Shwetank
jumped off and walked briskly in search of a campsite.

"Sir, excuse me," Beejgupta said to Mrityunjay. "I
had no idea it was so late. It must be tiring for you. On
the other hand, it is already past midnight. If you think
it is all right, we could keep going. We can break the
journey in the morning, when we reach a village, and
then rest for the day. That way we will save ourselves
from the afternoon heat."

"You are right, Beejgupta," Mrityunjay said. "It
does make sense to keep going."

Shwetank came back very soon, panting. He said,
"There is a very beautiful garden here, with a large
building. It is a courtier's land, and it has good arrangements for a halt."

"I remember now, I have stayed there," Mrityunjay
said. "The courtier's mansion is very nice."

The group turned towards the garden. A caretaker
received them warmly. Very soon, cots were laid for the
guests. The exhausted travellers were soon asleep—all
of them except for Beejgupta.

Where was he headed, and why? The questions re-
volved in Beejgupta's mind. He wanted to escape to Kashi,
to find peace, to get some respite from the thoughts that
tormented his mind in Patliputra, to make sure he did
not fail in his duties. He had wanted to be away from
Yashodhara, to pull himself apart from Chitralekha. But
Yashodhara had come even closer to him. Perhaps she
would not be much closer if they were united. "Impossible!" he cried out in his half-sleep. He could not bring
himself to love Yashodhara. Yashodhara faded from his
mind and Chitralekha took her place. Who was Chitralekha to him? What meaning did she bring into his
life? She was his beloved, his wife. He loved her, and she
loved him. But did she? Perhaps. Maybe not! Perhaps,
because she had left him for his good, because she had
accepted that it was for Beejgupta's good, in Kumargiri's presence. Perhaps not, because she had deserted him
against his wish, make his life a burden.

Beejgupta heard the chirping of the birds. The first
golden rays of the sun played with the morning breeze,
and the stars petered out, one after the other. In the
distance, Beejgupta saw Yashodhara playing with the
dewdrops on the jasmine flowers. He hoisted himself
out of the cot. He finished his morning chores and then
came back to enjoy the pleasant morning, thinking that
his overheated imagination would find some relaxation
there. Yashodhara called out to him. She held flowers in
her hand. "Arya Beejgupta," she said. "See how beautiful nature is here. There is so much joy, so much peace!
Far, far away from the worries, the desires, the curses of

the world, a pure life plays here with the multi-coloured wings of butterflies."

Beejgupta approached her, and stood next to her. He looked all around, and said, "Lady Yashodhara, I do not see any natural beauty around me."

"No?" Yashodhara asked. "Are you serious?"

"I am not joking," Beejgupta said. You say nature is beautiful. I say it is ugly."

Yashodhara was not willing to let that pass. "Look, this grass is so soft. I am tempted to sink into it, and stay here."

Beejgupta smiled. "Don't do that, lady Yashodhara," he said. "There is no doctor nearby if we need help. You say the grass is soft, it is beautiful, just because you have not been out in the open. Do you know how many insects there are in it? And it is damp. If you spend too much time rolling in it, you will get a cold. Unfortunately, nature is inconvenient and imperfect."

This was a new line of thinking for Yashodhara, and she did not have a retort ready. She asked, "So nature is imperfect?"

"Yes, it is. That is why man seeks refuge in the artificial. Like I said, the grass is beautiful and soft, but it is also damp and teeming with insects and spiders. Think of the bitter, ugly, foggy cold of these beautiful places in the winter. The terrible *loo*, the hot wind, dries up the skin in summer. Why did men start building homes, if not to protect themselves from the vagaries of nature? In our homes, our walls stop the northern winds and our fires produce enough heat to keep us warm. Curtains of *khus* grass, soaked in water, rout the dry summer heat.

Nature does not bother about human comfort—that makes it imperfect for us."

"But these flowers—how tender they are. Listen to the birdsong. How melodious it is, how fascinating. The cuckoo's call! How sweet, and full of compassion."

"The flowers are tender, but they also have thorns. And countless tiny insects throng the flowers. There softness and fragrance are ephemeral—what use are they? Their beauty withers away in solitude. And the songs of the birds—it may be sweet, but it is just the notes that are sweet. This chirping is an unemotional music. Where is the rise and fall of pitch? All the seven notes of music echo together. The human vocal chords produce superior music. And the cuckoo has only a repertoire of shrill, high notes that bore the mind if we listen to it for too long. No one knows what the cuckoo says. Perhaps it says nothing."

Yashodhara was taken aback by Beejgupta's vehemence. She had a garden in her mansion, and it gave her a small glimpse of nature. She had always been fascinated by nature, but now she realised that perhaps she had been deluded. There was an artificial fountain a little ahead of them. Near it, hoards of pigeons were bathing noisily in a man-made canal. Yashodhara walked towards the fountain, and Beejgupta accompanied her. She looked at the pigeons longingly. "How happy they are," she said softly. "How they play with each other. They don't have vices like jealousy, hatred or wickedness. I wish I had wings and I were a pigeon."

How simple she was, Beejgupta thought to himself. "Lady," he said, "if you were one, you would want to be a woman. You think they are happy and at peace, but you are wrong. They have enemies. Happiness is fulfilment of desires; sorrow is unfulfilled desires. Do you think the desires of these pigeons have been fulfilled? The question is whether they have desires in the first place. We humans are superior to birds and animals because we have desires and are happy to fulfil them. We are doers. We are not born to die after an inactive life. We are here on this earth to act. How wickedly birds and beasts fight for food. Remember, we have to labour for ours. We plough the land and produce wheat and grains, but the birds and beasts depend on nature's bounty. Birds devour insects, and animals eat each other. When their enemies, the eagles, pounce on these pigeons, think of their plight. How worried they are, how helpless."

Yashodhara looked at Beejgupta, surprised by his contrarian views. Beejgupta continued. "Lady Yashodhara, you probably think that the man who is one with nature is happy. Remember, man is never satisfied with his condition. You grew up in a palace. You take its beauty and its functionality for granted. Not only that, perhaps you feel the urge to free yourself from its bounds. You probably imagine an idyllic life in a hut near this nature that you see, and you may find the idea of a life in the open air of the village, surrounded by frolicking animals, very charming. It is natural for you to think that way. But do ask the villagers. They will say that happiness is in the palace, with maids and slaves at your command. Then again, our ancestors who built the first palaces must have been villagers once. Why did they establish cities? They did it to eliminate the ugliness and discomfort of nature through an unnatural, artificial approach to life. This garden that enchants you, is itself artificial. If you want nature, you must go into the jungle, where the lion roams free with its bloodthirsty tongue lolling out—where the tall grass hides venomous snakes that are ready to dispense a quick death to unwitting victims. Forget this artificial canal; think of the untamed river, where the deadly *ghariyal* crocodiles lurk in the muddy waters, ever ready to pounce on man. When you think all this through, you will realise whether there is more beauty and peace in nature or in the artificial world."

Yashodhara had looked at Beejgupta, surprised. She had thought of Beejgupta as a man of good character, but she now appreciated his intellect as well. She felt her admiration for him growing. "Arya Beejgupta," she said, "if I may ask, when and where did you read all this?"

"Lady, I have been taught by the school of the world, and the educational system of life. And now it seems it is time for breakfast—shall we?" They walked towards the mansion.

Beejgupta's unhappiness was writ large on his face. Yashodhara asked, "Arya Beejgupta, you are not happy. Will you tell me why?" She knew that she was provoking him.

Beejgupta took a deep breath. "Yes, lady Yashodhara, I am unhappy. But what good will it do you to know about it? You will be better off without knowing why."

"Is it a secret?"

"No, my life is open. I have no secrets, except those things that are inappropriate to divulge. In general, secrets are signs of fear, and fear is a sign of criminality. So, I do not keep secrets. On the other hand, I do think it inappropriate to make others unhappy with one's own sorrow."

Yashodhara was quiet. She felt that she had only saddened Beejgupta further by opening the topic. By this time, they had reached the main building, where Mrityunjay and Shwetank were waiting for them. Breakfast was ready.

Yashodhara ran to Mrityunjay and hugged him. "Father, today Arya Beejgupta told me things that opened my eyes," she said. "He proved my notions wrong. I did not know that he was so wise." She glanced at Beejgupta, and then she was drawn to Shwetank, who had turned pale. She reached out and held his trembling hand. "Arya Shwetank, are you unwell?" She started examining his pulse. "You do not have a fever," she pronounced. "Why do you look so pale?"

"It must be because he could not rest properly, and is exhausted," Beejgupta said. "Shwetank, you must rest today."

Yashodhara stood holding Shwetank's hand, and slowly his paleness disappeared. He said, "No I am not unwell. It's true I am a bit tired. I should be all right with some rest."

Later, after breakfast, Beejgupta checked with Shwetank if he wanted to sleep. Shwetank said that he was not sleepy. Beejgupta told him that he would take a nap, and asked Shwetank to wake him up before lunch.

He told Shwetank to spend time with Mrityunjay and Yashodhara, so that they did not feel ignored. Shwetank talked to Mrityunjay and Yashodhara. Yashodhara told them about the insights Beejgupta shared with her in the morning. Mrityunjay was impressed by Beejgupta's arguments. He asked Shwetank if Beejgupta was unwell.

Before Shwetank could reply, Yashodhara said, "Yes, I also thought so. I asked Beejgupta, and he admitted that he was sad, but he refused to tell me why." She looked at Shwetank.

"There are many things that are best kept secret," Mrityunjay said.

Yashodhara said, "I guess secrets represent man's dark side. Man will keep secrets for fear of being criticised and vilified by society. But I know Beejgupta's sorrow is not caused by a secret. He said so himself."

"And perhaps for Arya Beejgupta, secrets are linked with his dark side?" Shwetank said. He could not hide his sarcasm. "In fact, it is not always that way. Take my case. I am Arya Beejgupta's servant. His order is my duty. I have my individuality, but what of it? I am dependent on him. Some times the natural fire of rebellion consumes me. At such times, is it better to let the antagonism come out in the open, or to suppress it and carry out my duty? I think the answer is clear."

Mrityunjay said, "Young man, your antagonism is not appropriate, and it is best kept secret!"

Yashodhara said, "Yes, it is inappropriate, Arya Shwetank, and I feel sorry for you."

Shwetank saw a glow of love and sympathy in her eyes.

Chapter Sixteen

here are people who attract others towards them, only to dominate and enslave them. Chitralekha had this nature. She was not aware of this facet of her personality, but unknowingly she used it, and Kumargiri could not resist.

In his hut, Kumargiri and Chitralekha grew closer. Kumargiri wanted to distance himself from her, but to his surprise he always found himself next to her. She started living in the hut. When he meditated, she would come in and work there like a housewife. Kumargiri often found himself unable to focus. His eyes would flick open and he would see her. In an instant, he would close his eyes and try to focus his being, but it proved impossible.

As for Chitralekha, she had gone to Kumargiri's hut to love him. But once she was there, her feelings morphed. She was overcome by a desire to learn the discipline of meditation and austerity; she did not want to distract Kumargiri from his calling.

The lamp had been lit quite a while ago. It was two watches into the night. It was time for Kumargiri to meditate. He sat on his mat, in his usual position, but he could not concentrate.

Kumargiri opened his eyes when he heard Chitralekha's footsteps. "Lady Chitralekha," he said softly.

Chitralekha was startled. She had thought Kumargiri was absorbed in meditation. She rose and said, "Gurudeva, my apologies. I came in before you were completely focused. I shall leave, so that I do not disturb you."

Kumargiri smiled. "There is no need to leave. Please stay seated. Today I shall not go into a trance. I need to talk to you."

Chitralekha sat down.

"Chitralekha," Kumargiri said, "I was wondering if man can follow the paths of *karma*, action, and *dharma*, renunciation, simultaneously."

"I do not follow you."

"The day you came to me to ask for initiation, you said that you love me. Is that right?"

"Yes—and I was honest."

"And what does love mean?"

"Establishing a bond between two souls."

Kumargiri was silent for a few moments. "According to this definition, love can only be between two souls, and therefore between two human beings. So there cannot be love between human and Brahma, the creator?"

"But in your view, the soul is a part of *brahma*. So, the definition does not preclude love between human and *brahma*."

"I have thought of something new today, lady Chitralekha," Kumargiri said. "Celibacy is impossible for man, because it is negative. It is founded on void, emptiness. When one says that one is celibate, one is deluded, for in truth that one is detached only from the world of the senses, but attached to *brahma*. Life's work is creation, not destruction; man's duty is to be affectionate, not dispassionate. Love for *brahma* means ignorance of the other objects. So in reality, many men who are celibate, dispassionate and austere are in fact devoted and attached, but to *brahma*. This is not a very significant statement. What is more important is—are separation from the world and love of *brahma* one and the same thing?"

Chitralekha was worried. She knew Kumargiri's thought processes, and understood his weakness. She said, "Sir, I do not have an answer. I have come to get enlightened by the guru, to find a purpose in life, to know *brahma*."

Kumargiri lowered his head. His accumulated spiritual strength overpowered his sinful heart. "Lady, you are right," he said. "Enlightenment is not an object for argument. It is to be experienced. I myself do not know why this evil line of thought emerged from my mind, but it now has a life of its own. The question haunts me:

is it possible to love God while being indifferent to the world? I shall not find peace till I have answered it."

Chitralekha looked within herself, and found a strange transformation in her mind. She had set off to love Kumargiri. But now, she found that she could not love him, she could not worship him…she could not learn from him. The turbulent life of the city now repulsed her; the recluse's life with its peace, its glow of purity, attracted her. The joys of the sensual life bored her; too much happiness pained her. The pacific atmosphere of Kumargiri's hut satiated and calmed her.

Kumargiri kept his thoughts to himself for some time. Then he spoke: "Lady Chitralekha, I have not understood you yet. But my heart tells me that we will be together for a long time."

This was what Chitralekha had thought when she came to Kumargiri. "Perhaps," she said, "but my past clouds my thinking so much that I cannot see into the future."

Kumargiri sighed. "It is possible I am wrong, but tell me one thing truly. You have a powerful attraction. Where did you get this power?"

Chitralekha's face turned red. It had been many years since she had blushed like a shy girl. She avoided Kumargiri's eyes and searched for the right words. "Gurudeva, I did not know that I have it."

Kumargiri stood up and paced the room. He said, "I cannot concentrate today. Why is it so hard for me to focus on the formless?" His words came out louder now. "Why? My heart pounds and says, 'Think of the beauty of form!'" He fixed his gaze on Chitralekha. "Dancer, till this day I have worshipped the formless. Now I want to understand form. I want to carry out an experiment. You will help me perform it."

Chitralekha shivered. She saw a dim shadow cover Kumargiri. His usually beatific face was distorted. She was frightened by the blazing fire she had ignited in the yogi. She stood up, and felt her energy drain away.

Kumargiri held Chitralekha's hands. Chitralekha shivered from head to toe. The yogi's hands felt like red hot iron. His body was aflame. "I am adopting the worship of form, dancer! You instigated this want in my heart, and you will have to support this experiment—you will be the target, understand?"

Chitralekha understood all too well. This was what she had come for. But it was not as she had imagined it. She had wanted a gentle, scented, sandalwood breeze; she did not want to be burnt by a volcano.

Kumargiri held her tight in the grip of his embrace. His lips sought out Chitralekha's. He withdrew a bit to say, "Dancer! I love you!"

Chitralekha was scorched by his hot breath. With an effort, she pulled her face away from Kumargiri's. "Gurudeva, you are going astray," she said. "You are giving up many years of spiritual seeking."

Kumargiri's hands went limp. He stepped back. The madness in his eyes disappeared in a moment, and his face turned pale. "What was I doing?" he said in a hoarse whisper. "Excuse me, lady." He stormed out of the room.

Chitralekha slumped and sat on her mat. She had come to Kumargiri—and now she wanted to leave him.

She collapsed on the ground and sobbed like a child. She was pained that she had gone so far astray. She had fallen herself, and dragged another down with her. She fell into a troubled sleep.

Kumargiri was wandering in the open. A while ago, his body had burned feverishly and the sensation was delicious. Now it was his mind that burned, and he felt only nausea. How hard he had fallen, and how fast, from the pinnacle that he had reached after years of rigour! It was his duty to win over his weakness.

Ahead of him, there was an immense darkness. The lights of Patliputra glimmered faintly in the distance. His feet took him towards the dark. "I cannot stop. My fall is definite. I must save myself somehow," he muttered.

He had walked quite far from his hut. An inner voice called out to him: "Aren't you a coward?"

He stopped.

"Where do you think you are going?" the voice continued. "Triumphing over weakness is the biggest proof of spiritual prowess. Until you master yourself, you are incomplete. And that is why Chitralekha has come to you—so that you can remove a chink in your spiritual armour. Are you scared of her? She does not lead you to your fall. You only have your weakness to blame for it. Do away with it! You have the moral energy of the sage. Why do you retreat?"

"I will stand and fight," Kumargiri whispered. He turned around. When he reached the hut, Chitralekha lay in a crumpled sleep. In that dim light, he could see the tear marks on her cheeks. Kumargiri knelt by her head and gazed at her for a long time. Then he bent towards her face, and saw her face ease into a smile. He placed his lips on hers—but he jerked back the moment they touched. Her lips were cool.

He moved to his mat, and sat there in the lotus position. He tried to concentrate, but it was no use. Exhausted, he lowered himself and lay down. His last conscious thought was that he must become his own master again.

CHAPTER SEVENTEEN

hen Chitralekha woke up, morning had broken but Kumargiri was still asleep instead of being in meditation. She walked outside. Her head was heavy, and she felt shattered. Her sleep had been fitful, and her heartbeat was unsteady.

The first sun rays had pierced the canopy of the forest. The gentle morning breeze, slowed down by fresh flower bloom, carried the songs of the birds to her. All these gave her no respite from her unease. She saw Vishaldeva meditating under a banyan tree.

Chitralekha took a breath and tried to order her panicked thoughts. Was it right for her to continue to stay in Kumargiri's hut? But where could she go? With what face could she go to Beejgupta? And would Beejgupta even accept her? She had no idea. She had trudged to where Vishaldeva sat immersed in a meditative trance.

He heard her steps, opened his eyes, and greeted her with a respectful *namaste*.

She responded by joining her palms.

"Does the lady have something to tell me?" Vishaldeva asked, looking curiously at her.

"Indeed I do," Chitralekha said. "And it is very important. But before I say anything, you must promise me that if you cannot accept my request, you will keep it to yourself. I will speak after you make this promise."

"I promise."

"Listen, Vishaldeva, I was wrong to come here. I came here to rise to a higher plane, but I only find myself falling."

Vishaldeva smiled. "I see."

Chitralekha saw the contempt in his smile, and it made her shake with fury. She spoke in a low, controlled voice. "You laugh, because you do not believe me. I know you saw Kumargiri and me together that night. I might as well tell you—I cannot do what I came here to do. I see now that I should not have followed this path. I have fallen, but I will not debase myself any more. And I am also dragging Kumargiri down with me. That is a great sin. Will you help me atone for my sin?"

"I am here for you."

"Do you know Arya Beejgupta's place?"

"Yes."

"A young man named Shwetank lives with him. Tell him I want to see him."

"Very well."

They saw Kumargiri stepping out of his hut, and stopped talking. Kumargiri walked up to them and stood with his head lowered, like a criminal. The three of them were silent for a few moments. Kumargiri broke the silence. "I overslept today," he said. "I am sorry." He went past them.

Vishaldeva looked at Chitralekha. "Lady, the guru does not look well today."

"Yes, the guru is not well, and my presence here is what makes him unwell. Vishaldeva, you have to help me—not for my sake, but for your master's."

"I will help you. I will go to Beejgupta's place today."

Kumargiri did not return to his hut that day. Vishaldeva returned from Patliputra in the evening and told Chitralekha that Beejgupta had gone on a pilgrimage to Kashi.

Chitralekha felt enervated. "What do we do now?" she asked Vishaldeva.

"I don't understand at all."

"You don't understand at all. Nor do I. This is the irony of destiny." She stopped. She stood quiet for some time. Her eyes looked as if she was searching for a distant point. "Or maybe it is the fruit of my sins. I had a harbour. I left it. I forsook Beejgupta. Why? Not for nothing. I came here for enlightenment. Is this it? God is giving me knowledge. But what is all this? Vishaldeva! There is nothing you can do. The great guru cannot do anything, nor can I. What has to happen, will happen." Her eyes became wild, and her face distorted. She trembled with excitement.

Vishaldeva cowered when he saw her take this form. He said, "Lady, can you not go back to where you came from? From where you were in your earlier life?"

Chitralekha smiled. "My earlier life? Don't be a fool. I have moved on, and I did not move on just to go back. Retreating would be cowardly. It would defy nature. Who can go back in this world? Who has ever done it? We reach the jaws of death moving forward instant by instant—would we not be immortal if we could retreat from death? Forward! That is the iron law of life. In virtue and in sin, we only move forward. Do you understand?" She walked away without another word, leaving Vishaldeva staring at her receding form.

Chitralekha walked towards Kumargiri, who was seated in the shadow of a wall of creepers. Kumargiri stood up when he saw her approaching. "The Guru did not come to his hut today?" Chitralekha asked.

"True, I did not, dancer. Going in there today—oh, it terrifies me!"

"Yes, but what must we do about it?"

"You ask what we must do? There is just one remedy. I have become a worshipper of form, but I cannot perform the worship without you."

"The worship of form is a delusion!"

"It is not for you to decide that, dancer! You are my disciple. It is your duty to obey me." Kumargiri stood upright before her.

Chitralekha did not flinch. She replied with the same firmness. "Yogi, do not forget that the woman in front of you is not so helpless that you can rule her. You think you have initiated me. You are the one who is deluded. You deceive yourself. Who are you to order me? Do you not know that you have made yourself a slave of the one whom you want to order around?"

Kumargiri sighed and sat down, bent. "Dancer, I love you." His voice was hoarse and pitiful.

Chitralekha laughed, and said, "I know you love me. But I do not love you any more! For a moment, I wanted to rule you, I tried to. I succeeded. But what of that? For a woman to rule a man is not a sign of love. Nature has not made women rulers of men. Nature has made them to be won over, to give themselves to their men. A woman cannot love a man weaker than her. A man whom she rules cannot be a claimant to her love. Woman must surrender herself to her lover, fuse her being with her lover's. The one who wins her over, who rules her, can love her, Yogi! Here is the crux: a man's love is to rule over his lover. A woman's love is to surrender herself to her lover. Here I am the mistress, and you the slave. I have won you over. You have surrendered. What right do you have to my love?"

Kumargiri heard her out in silence. What she said was true, though it was bitter. He realised how weak he had been, and he sensed the enormity of his defeat. He breathed deeply and thought for some time. Then he stood up. The paleness of his face had disappeared, and the light was back in his eyes.

"You are right," he said. "I surrendered to you, and I turned out to be weaker than you. The Almighty used you to shatter my pride, to make me realise how tiny I am. Now I will take charge. I will win you over, not to love you, but to rule you. To save myself from the fall. Believe me, you will not find me so weak again."

Chitralekha said, "I can help you."

"How?"

"I want to leave. I have been an obstacle in your path."

"That is impossible, dancer! You cannot leave. Who will I win over if you are not around? You must stay. Is that clear?"

"Yogi, you have to master yourself, not me. You will not be able to do that while I am here. This I know. Your well-being is in my leaving."

Kumargiri's face turned red. "No! You will stay. You underestimate my strength. If you are gone, the conflict will be gone. How will I win? I need a way to test myself. Your presence here is essential. God has sent you to me. I failed once; there was a time when I did not know failure. I must find my old form. I will not let you go till I have completely succeeded in this battle."

"Not let me go? Can you stop me?"

"No," Kumargiri spoke in a softer tone. "Perhaps no one in the world can stop you. The weak cannot stop the mighty. I can only pray to you, request you. You do accept that you are responsible for my fall."

"I have not made you fall. You fell yourself. Perhaps I played a role, that is all."

"Well, I fell myself, and I shall rise myself. But you were the instrument of my fall. Can you not be the means of my rising?"

Chitralekha's mouth was dry. She lowered her eyes. "You are right. I can."

"Will you not accept my request? Can you not stay for some time, and let me restore my spiritual energy?"

Chitralekha thought for a few moments before replying. "How much time do you want me to grant you?"

"Grant? If I do succeed in my mission, will you still object to staying with me? In any case, if I win, I will know that I am on the right path. And you will know the rightful path as well."

"No, I already know I cannot follow your path. But I will stay for now. If I feel like leaving, I will let you know. You will not be able to stop me then."

CHAPTER EIGHTEEN

hitralekha had left Beejgupta's life against his will. Yashodhara entered it without his permission. Beejgupta found his life a bitter joke.

He had wanted to drown his heart's turmoil in the bustle of Kashi, but he could not. Yashodhara's image flickered in front of his eyes instead of Chitralekha's. A faint happiness had taken a grip on him.

Beejgupta and his companions had been nearly a week in Kashi. It was evening. They sat together, taking in the scenic beauty of the city. "I would settle down here, Mrityunjay said. "It is only the web of family duties that keeps me away."

Beejgupta parried him. "Arya, the difference between the worldly and the celibate, the householder and the sage is not all that it is made out to be." He chuckled at Mrityunjay's incredulous expression. "You may find this strange, sir, but I do believe it to be true."

Shwetank saw an opening. Taking Mrityunjay's side, he said, "Master, who knows what the truth is? Truth is another name for what is appropriate in the circumstances, and circumstances are ever shifting."

A faint smile played on Mrityunjay's face. "Young man, you may be right, but you do not enlighten me about Beejgupta's assertion. So, Beejgupta, can you help me understand you?"

Beejgupta was hurt by Shwetank's unsolicited remark. He spoke a bit harshly. "Well it should be self-evident. Man can never be dispassionate. Dispassion stands for death. What we see as the dispassion of the sage is just a different form of passion. Passion is desire; dispassion is contentment." Beejgupta's eyes met Yashodhara's.

Silence reigned for some time. It was a silence tinged with sorrow. Shwetank was the only one whose mind worked furiously. He realised he had sinned by rushing to counter Beejgupta.

Yashodhara saw that Shwetank was crestfallen. She understood what was worrying him. She tried to change the subject. "Arya Beejgupta, how long will you stay here?"

"I cannot say," Beejgupta said. "At times I long for Patliputra, but the very next moment I resist the thought of leaving Kashi." He turned to Mrityunjay. "Sir, what are your plans?"

Mrityunjay looked at Yashodhara, and said, "It is not up to me. I came here at Yashodhara's wish. We will stay as long as she wishes."

Beejgupta looked at Yashodhara smiling, and for the first time, in that soft light, he saw her as the magically beautiful young woman that she was. She held his gaze. Mrityunjay looked away.

Shwetank found the moment oppressive. "Master, do you not plan to go out sightseeing tonight?" he blurted out.

Beejgupta was startled. He looked away from Yashodhara, and Yashodhara turned to Shwetank. "Arya," Beejgupta asked Mrityunjay, "what do you think?"

"I am not keen on going out tonight," Mrityunjay said.

Shwetank asked Yashodhara, "Lady Yashodhara, will you come?"

"What's the point of wasting time sitting here?" Yashodhara said with a laugh.

"I do not feel up to it, either," Beejgupta said.

"Then does Arya Shwetank have your permission to accompany me?" Yashodhara asked.

"Surely." Beejgupta was forced into the polite reply.

Yashodhara and Shwetank left.

Beejgupta remained with Mrityunjay. "Arya, you had plans to perform a *yagya* here—have your plans changed?"

"Yes, I have postponed the plans," Mrityunjay said. "Arya Beejgupta, I have been thinking about this problem and have not been able to resolve it—is it impossible to remove animal sacrifice from our *yagyas*?"

"Why do you ask?" Beejgupta said. "I hope the minister has not been influenced by the talk of the Buddhist monks?"

"What if I have? Is there a point to all this blood-shed? Doesn't it trigger disgust towards the faith? The Buddha's sermons are not without meaning."

"And not without truth," Beejgupta said softly. He got up and stretched. "Arya, I have changed my mind. Do you object to stepping out for a walk?"

"I only said I wasn't too keen. I don't have any objection either. Let's go."

In a short while, they were in Mrityunjay's chariot. Tired of the noise of the city, he turned the chariot towards the Ganga. A row of boats was lined up, ready to leave. Beejgupta saw Shwetank and Yashodhara about to climb on to one of them. Beejgupta called out, "Shwetank!"

Shwetank was gazing at the boats rocking on the Ganga. He did not hear Beejgupta. Yashodhara spoke to him. "Look, father and Beejgupta are here."

Shwetank turned his head away. By then the chariot had stopped and the two men had stepped down. Shwetank's face fell. "Curse him!" he said softly—but Yashodhara heard him.

"Arya Shwetank, control is an important part of life," Yashodhara chided him.

He could see she was serious, and he flinched. "It's just that control and romance do not mix well."

Mrityunjay and Beejgupta were with them by now. Shwetank's disappointment was writ large on his face, and Beejgupta did not fail to notice it. "Shwetank, we didn't feel comfortable after you both left. So here we are."

Shwetank laughed a cursory laugh. "I had asked the master to join us."

They climbed on to the boat, and their boat joined the multitude of others floating in the currents of the river. They were surrounded by musical performances and cheerful conversation.

"Arya Shwetank, do you find Kashi beautiful, or Patliputra?" Yashodhara asked.

Shwetank pondered the question for a while, and said, "I think I prefer Patliputra. Kashi does not have the grandeur of Patliputra. It is more a centre of learning and education."

"And you, Beejgupta?"

"These days I prefer Kashi."

"Why these days?" Yashodhara asked again.

"Lady Yashodhara, a place has circumstances associated with it. We actually don't like places—they are lifeless. We like the soul, the environment, of a place, the things that we are used to and that are parts of our life. Each of us likes the place where we were born and where we grew up. We have friends where we belong. Our lives are not made up of our conscious selves, which are shaped by the people we have contact with. Given all this, it would be natural for me to like Patliputra more than Kashi, but there is a bit more to it than that. The same set of circumstances does not appeal to a person all the time. We need change as well, and it helps to be surrounded by new circumstances. The new circumstances appeal to us till the time our craving for change is satisfied. I am not yet done with Kashi; I still like it more than Patliputra."

Yashodhara smiled. "Arya Beejgupta," she said, "you have a remarkable intellect. Your arguments are infallible." She turned to Shwetank. "And Arya Shwetank, you must not fall into arguing against this knowledge. You have to watch out for Arya Beejgupta."

"Well I am Arya Beejgupta's class-fellow; we have the same guru, the revered Ratnambar," Shwetank said with a grin. "I suppose I should also watch out for the guru?"

"I can't presume to advise you about the guru." Yashodhara asked.

"Why can't you?" Beejgupta said. "You can say what you think is right. Why be shy?"

"There is nothing to be shy about," Yashodhara said. "It is just that I know you very well and I feel close to you. The great Ratnambar seems forbidding and holy."

Beejgupta's eyes met Yashodhara's, and they looked at each other without blinking. Yashodhara's eyes showed no sign of shyness or hesitation. They were clear, and innocent. Beejgupta felt his blood surge and his heart quicken. He willed himself to look away, and his eyes met Shwetank's. Shwetank's eyes told him that Shwetank could sense what was happening to him. He felt a flush of anger at himself, and at Shwetank.

"Shwetank!"

"Master?"

Beejgupta got control of himself before he spoke. "Nothing... How many days have we been here?" he asked.

Shwetank guessed that Beejgupta had made an effort to head off the words that were welling up inside him. He counted the days in his mind, and said, "Eight days."

"I think it is time to head back to Patliputra," he said. Then he spoke in a whisper, so that only Shwetank could hear him. "It is impossible to forget Chitralekha. Make arrangements for us to return."

Shwetank was pleased at this sudden about turn, and Mrityunjay and Yashodhara were puzzled. "Does Arya Beejgupta really wish to head back?" Mrityunjay asked.

Beejgupta bowed his head. "Arya Mrityunjay, please forgive me. One of my vices is that I am very dependent on my inspirations and whims. I do now know at any time what I will feel like doing in an hour. Right now, my memories of Patliputra came calling, and I felt an overpowering urge to leave Kashi."

"So when do you wish to leave?" Yashodhara asked. "We will also have to prepare ourselves. Arya Beejgupta, inspiration and whim are all very well, but you do need to think about the convenience of others."

Beejgupta looked shamefaced. "You are right, lady. Your convenience comes first. We will go when it suits you."

"No, that's not what I meant," Yashodhara said. "I made a general statement. If it is all right, let us leave tomorrow evening. We have to buy some things, and I will go with Arya Shwetank to get them at the market tomorrow."

CHAPTER NINETEEN

eejgupta was surprised at himself. Without willing it, he found himself attracted to Yashodhara. He may even have accepted her if he had not been warned off by the hurt he saw on Shwetank's face.

He came to Kashi to forget his sorrow, to calm the turbulence that raged within him. He thought his wound would not heal as long as he continued his opulent life in Patliputra, with Chitralekha in proximity. The thought propelled him to leave his hometown like an aimless traveller.

But, he reflected, was he aimless? Was anyone aimless, and was it possible to be aimless? Perhaps. Beejgupta's mind floundered. On the other hand, did man have a goal? Could a man say what he came into this world for, what he wanted to do and what he would do? Not really. Man was an instrument. He was the slave of circumstance; he was aimless. An unknown power drove mankind. Human desire had no value. Humans were not independent. They were not doers. They were the means.

Beejgupta tossed in his sleep. It was past midnight, and the night was still. He started thinking again. "Tomorrow I go to Patliputra. Why? To meet Chitralekha. To draw her back to me." He was confident that if he insisted on it, Chitralekha would not refuse him. "No, I will not go to her. Why should I? Did I leave her? No, she left me. Why? Perhaps that was destiny's will. But if it was, then it cannot be erased. Why should I grieve? Let her go. Why should I spoil my life?"

Beejgupta closed his eyes and tried to sleep, but his thoughts hammered away at him. "Do sacrifice and pain destroy life? Is sorrow not a part of life? Does fate grant happiness to everyone? No. Sorrow is as important as happiness. So I should bear sorrow—I should embrace the path of sacrifice. I should perform my duty. And what is my duty?"

Beejgupta dragged himself out of bed, and drank a glass of water. He washed his face and went back to lie down.

"So what is my duty?" he thought. "I was born to act. It is my duty to lead a family life, to grow my family. This means I must get married. Perhaps that is why Chitralekha left me? So I marry, and experience domestic life... And there is a suitable partner. Yashodhara! Her beauty is no less than Chitralekha's. She is a jewel, an idol of purity. Will I have to marry her? She has all the qualities desirable in a woman. So be it. But is it possible? I have already turned her down once. What right do I have to ask Mrityunjay for her hand now? It is quite possible that great courtier may refuse to give her to me." Beejgupta shook his head. "No! Impossible! I cannot think of marrying Yashodhara now. It is too late—much too late. Chitralekha... Only Chitralekha can share my life now."

Beejgupta got up again, reconciling himself to the fact that he would not sleep that night. He looked out a window at the moonlit sky. There were two watches left before morning. He stepped out of the house and walked to the shore of the Ganga. Three men sat on the shore, engaged in a lively discussion. Beejgupta took a seat near them.

The one who was talking was a grizzled old man of about seventy. He had a kindly face lined with wrinkles. His discourse marked him out as a sage. To his right sat a thin man of about twenty-five. He was of medium build, and his forehead was lined with worry. A fat man of about fifty sat to the sage's left. This man had a bushy beard and his hair had started greying.

The sage was speaking. "You are not of the right age for you to become an ascetic. Go follow the call of duty and obey your father."

The young man gripped the sage's feet. "I ask for shelter. Please accept me and initiate me into the ascetic life. I have no attachment to a worldly life. The worldly life requires an objective. Now that I have developed this distance from the sensuous world, I will only harm myself if I try to be a part of it. I will never find peace. You can ask my father how painful the last two years have been for me."

"Yes," the young man's father said, "but that is because you do not listen to me. I have said, again and
again, that you must remarry. You are still young. Life
and death will go on. You do not have a child. It is simply not appropriate for you to become a recluse. You will
find attachment once you settle into matrimony."

"Your father is right," the sage said. "Son, love is a
figment of the imagination. The man-woman relationship happens only in this world. Outside of this world,
they are different souls. Even in this world, the union
of the souls is not possible. Love is just an affinity of
the souls. This affinity is not as significant as it is made
out to be. It can be broken, as you have experienced.
Drowning your life in sorrow is not the proper way to
respond. Your duty is to marry. By not marrying, you
shirk your duty."

"How so?"

"Listen. Woman is weak. It is man's duty to give
her shelter. Marriage is the means by which man does
so. If man did not shelter woman, her position would be
pitiable. On the other hand, man would also face many
difficulties. When you think of renunciation and asceticism, you are being a coward. You are going against
your duty to protect a weak woman."

The young man replied, "But master, I want only to
purify myself in the fire of austerity after giving up the
pleasures of the world. Where is the cowardice in this?"

The sage smiled. "You want to bake yourself in fire
of austerity. Why? Just because you loved, and the love
went out of your life. But your meditation will be of no
use. It will be suicidal. You are not motivated by a higher

purpose; you are wallowing in self-pity and you are on the path to self-destruction."

The young man prostrated himself and touched the sage's feet with his head. "I accept your command." His father bowed as well, and they left.

Beejgupta bowed his head before the sage. The sage smiled and asked, "So, do you want to become as ascetic as well?"

"No, sir," Beejgupta said "I have no such plans. I enjoyed hearing you speak, and that is why I sat listening to you."

"Well," the sage said, "the man who comes to the Ganga at this hour, if he is not a pauper or a sage, must be a troubled man."

"You are right, master," Beejgupta said. "My dilemma is uncommon. Your words have given me some insight into the issues that trouble me. May I ask you some questions?"

"Of course! With pleasure."

"You just said that it was suicidal for that young man to sacrifice his life at the altar of unsuccessful love. But is it not natural to feel the prick of the memory of a lost love? Is it not destructive to one's soul to suppress the resulting pain, or to use artificial means to forget it?"

The sage was silent for some time. Then he began: "You are right in what you said. Sorrow dilutes itself with time. Humans of different natures need differing time intervals to recover from sadness. Using artificial means to speed up this recovery is unnatural, of course. But remember this: not every unnatural behaviour is harmful to the soul. We have adopted artificiality so

much that it has become natural. Wearing clothes is unnatural, the food we eat is unnatural, our partaking of
sensual pleasures is unnatural, the glamour around us is
unnatural. Natural life is a burden—we lighten it with
sports and spectacles, dance and drama, and festivals.
And now these are what we claim give meaning to our
lives. Drowning sorrow with artificial means is not destructive. It may be unnatural, but it is also instinctive."

"I thank you, sir," Beejgupta said as he got up. "You
have lifted a burden off my mind. You have made me
capable of realising my duty. Farewell.

The morning breeze caressed Beejgupta's skin. A
faint light had appeared in the Eastern sky and flights
of birds announced themselves. Beejgupta reached his
room—and fell asleep.

When he awoke, it was afternoon. Yashodhara and
Shwetank were out shopping. Beejgupta finished with
his daily chores and went to Mrityunjay.

"Arya Beejgupta, you rose very late today. Did you
not sleep well at night?"

"I'm afraid I did not. I could not keep from thinking all night."

"What about?"

"About my future."

Mrityunjay smiled a restrained smile. "After Chitralekha left a vacuum in your life, it is natural to you to
think about your future. Arya Beejgupta, did you come
to a conclusion?"

Beejgupta felt scalded by the undertone of sarcasm
in Mrityunjay's words. He stopped himself from being

too frank, and spoke in a guarded way: "No, I did not, but I believe I will decide soon."

"I know what you will decide, Arya Beejgupta. I believe I have learned to recognise the inner inclinations of men."

Beejgupta tried to change the topic. "Arya, you must have ordered your servants to make arrangements for the journey."

"Yes, and I have also asked Shwetank to order your servants to do the same."

"You have done well, sir."

Yashodhara's voice carried through to them. "Arya Shwetank, if father does not like this necklace, you will have to return it. I bought it at your insistence." She entered as she finished these words.

She saw Beejgupta and said, "Arya Beejgupta, we left you sleeping. See I have brought so many things—but I bought nothing for you."

"I do not need anything," Beejgupta said with a smile.

"Well, I did not need anything either, but I had to take some souvenirs," Yashodhara said, and she started unpacking the shopping baskets.

"How is this?" she asked, placing a jewelled necklace in his hand.

"It is nice, but it must be expensive."

"Yes, it is. But I have not purchased it yet. I only brought it here to show it to father."

Mrityunjay took the necklace and held it up in the light. "If you like it, buy it," he said.

Yashodhara showed her other acquisitions. All of them were approved. Beejgupta looked at Shwetank. "Did you not buy anything?"

"I did not ask the master," Shwetank said. "And besides, I do not need anything."

"No, you should have got something for yourself. We must set this right. I will come with you." He turned to Yashodhara. "Lady Yashodhara, if you do not mind, will you come back to the market? I will also buy somethings for myself, and I will need your assistance."

"I can come, but after eating. I am very tired now."

After lunch, Beejgupta asked Mrityunjay, "Arya, will you join us?"

"No, I am too old," Mrityunjay said. "The hubbub of the city does not attract me any more."

Beejgupta went to the market with Shwetank and Yashodhara. They stopped at a jeweller's shop first. Beejgupta and Shwetank took diamond rings for themselves. Beejgupta saw Yashodhara staring at a pearl necklace. He asked for it to be taken out of its case.

"Lady Yashodhara, what do you think?"

"It is beautiful. I did not see this when we came in the morning. If I had, I would have taken this rather than the jewelled one." She looked at Shwetank with a naughty smile. "Arya Shwetank, this happened because of you."

Beejgupta took the necklace from the jeweller, and fastened it around Yashodhara's neck. "Lady, this is a gift," he said.

Yashodhara trembled from head to feet at Bee-jgupta's delicate touch. She took the necklace off, and said, "Arya Beejgupta, I cannot accept this without my father's permission." Her voice was thick with emotion.

Beejgupta took the necklace. "Lady, you should not have any objection to accepting my gift. But you are right to wait for your father's approval."

CHAPTER TWENTY

umargiri was surprised at Chitralekha. She was the one who was so keen to come to him; he had not been attracted to her. Why the change in her attitude, he asked himself.

He was even more surprised at himself. He had tried his level best to keep Chitralekha away. What made him come to accept her presence now? Was it his desire to triumph over his own disbelief? Was it his belief that fate held only victory for him—the disappointment of defeat was a new sensation for him. Perhaps he knew his weakness, and he had accepted her to stamp out this weakness. He tried, and he failed. And what an ignominious failure it was! He let himself down, but even worse, he had lost to an ordinary dancer. His fall saddened him, but his anger overrode his sadness. "No, I must win Chitralekha. But how?" he asked himself.

"Why does she not love me?" he reasoned. "Perhaps because she loves another man. If she forgets her love for Beejgupta, perhaps—no, certainly—she will surrender herself to me. Beejgupta must be removed from her path."

Chitralekha had spent more than two months with Kumargiri. It was a month since their last active encounter. Since then, Kumargiri had controlled himself. He did not allow the slightest display of weakness. On some days, he had thought that he could free himself from the desire to possess her, even in her presence. But this feeling did not last. The fire that was lit demanded an oblation.

Kumargiri asked Chitralekha to sit next to him. "Lady Chitralekha, it has been a month. I have tried to uplift myself. I think I have rid myself of my weak chink."

"That is possible," Chitralekha said with a smile.

"I have heard that Arya Beejgupta has gone on a trip to Kashi," Kumargiri said. "Arya Mrityunjay and his daughter have accompanied him."

"So Yashodhara has gone with Beejgupta?" Chitralekha asked. Her smile disappeared.

This time Kumargiri smiled. "What is surprising about that? Lady Chitralekha, you left Beejgupta saying that he should marry Yashodhara and enter domestic life—you did right. Is Arya Beejgupta not doing the right thing if he marries Yashodhara?"

"I don't know… I don't know!" Chitralekha said in a loud and choked voice. "Please don't talk to me about Beejgupta."

"So I should not talk about Beejgupta? Why? Because you love him? You can't bear the thought of his love for another woman? If so, why did you leave him? Perhaps you think that woman has the right to do as she pleases, but not man. Or do you think that Beejgupta is your slave?"

Kumargiri's words were tinged with his desire for revenge. He wanted to defeat this woman who had defeated him.

"What I did, I did for Beejgupta well-being!" Chitralekha trembled with emotion. "In the eyes of society, I was responsible for his downfall. I left him so that he could rise again by conforming to social mores."

"How can I accept that, lady Chitralekha? You deceive yourself. When you forsook Beejgupta, you did it to love me!" Kumargiri's tone was admonishing. Kumargiri felt within himself the same old freshness, his past vigour, his lost gravitas, all of which had deserted him when Chitralekha came into his life. "You can fool Beejgupta; you can fool me. But you cannot fool yourself. You rejected pure love because you were possessed by lust. You saw something in me, and you became attracted to me. Your animal instinct overpowered your humanity. You came to me against Beejgupta's wish, and made his life a burden for him. And this is a man who sacrificed his prospects of family life to be able to give you, a dancer, a love that was pure and came from the depths of his heart."

"Stop it! Stop!" Chitralekha shrieked.

Kumargiri stared Chitralekha down. He laughed. "I should stop?" he said. "I only talked a bit and it has made you restless, dancer. No, I will finish what I have to say and you will hear me out. You will get the fruit of your actions. You think Beejgupta still loves you—you think he will accept you when he returns and you go back to him? If that is what you think, you are wrong. He has found the antidote to your poison. You did everything in your power to destroy him, but Yashodhara has rescued him, and now Beejgupta is enjoying conjugal life with her."

"Are you telling the truth, yogi?" Chitralekha asked. "Has Beejgupta married Yashodhara? No, yogi, that is not possible!"

"Not possible?" Kumargiri's sarcasm was piercing. "Your coming to me, driven by lust, rejecting your lover's true love, is possible. And Beejgupta's establishment of a pure relationship with a noble lady is not? Oh, you have such delusions, so much self-confidence! If you do not believe me, go and see for yourself. The newly-married couple have arrived in town this morning. You can go and congratulate them. You can see your lover—no, your slave—loving another woman with your own eyes."

"So they have come?" Chitralekha stood up. She was trembling, and her face had lost its colour. She looked towards Patliputra. "Have they really come back? Yogi, I beg you, please just say that you lied to me."

"Say that it is not true?" Kumargiri burst out laughing and the peals echoed in the hut. "Say that the truth is a lie? Go! Go and see for yourself."

Chitralekha staggered and sat down in a heap. "No, it is all over. I will not go now. What use is it. I have lost everything I had." Her voice was hoarse.

Kumargiri went closer to her. "It is all over? An ending can be the beginning for something new. How is it all over, lady Chitralekha?" Kumargiri's words were mellifluous now. "You know I love you. And even if you do not love me, you do not hate me either. You want to be in my life—before, Beejgupta was an obstacle. But you gave him sorrow, and he repaid you. Beejgupta found a pillar of support for himself, but you do not need to look far for yours. Lady Chitralekha, I love you!" Kumargiri took Chitralekha's hand.

Chitralekha let him take her hand without resisting. She raised her head and looked straight into his eyes.

"Love! love is my new faith! You came into my life—you did it to initiate me into this faith. Come, unite with me!"

Kumargiri's bowed his face a bit, and Chitralekha raised hers. Their lips met, and remained locked for a long time.

Kumargiri was ranting softly, like a possessed man. "You have come to drown me, and I am ready to drown! Let us start. Ah, these tremors... what peace, what pleasure! My deity, mistress of my life, I want to drink the elixir of your youth!" He closed his eyes, and Chitralekha closed her teary eyes as well. They embraced and felt each other's warmth.

"Take me," Chitralekha said.

When Chitralekha opened her eyes in the morning, she was anxious. The thought that Beejgupta had forsaken her rankled deeply. She cursed herself for leaving Beejgupta.

Kumargiri was sleeping and his breaths were deep. His face was distorted. The lust that had possessed him seemed to have cast a pall on the vigour that had once exuded. Chitralekha gazed at him for a long time, and then shivered without a reason. She could not stay there any longer. She stepped out of the hut. Why had that man's face seemed so ugly and frightful, just after a night of passion? She was surprised at her feelings.

Vishaldeva was returning from his prayers, and he saw Chitralekha and greeted her. "Why is the lady so glum?" he asked.

"I had dreadful dreams all night long," Chitralekha said with a forced smile. "They disturbed me."

"Has the guru not come out?" Vishaldeva asked.

"He is still in his trance," Chitralekha said.

"In his trance!" Vishaldeva exclaimed. "He has broken his discipline for the first time ever!"

They were silent for some time. Vishaldeva asked softly, "Lady Chitralekha, may I ask you about those dreams?"

"I think it is enough to say that they had to do with my past life."

"Past life?" Vishaldeva thought for a few moments. "Lady, if you think it proper, I can find out about Arya Beejgupta. It impossible that he has returned."

"Oh he has. I know. But what about it? His being back makes no difference to me."

Vishaldeva looked askance at her. "Lady, you make no sense. I don't understand you. The other day you wanted to go to him."

Chitralekha's face flushed red. "Yes, the other day I wanted to go. Today I do not. Have you considered how inappropriate it is for you to take such interest in my private life?"

Vishaldeva lowered his head. "You are right, lady. But showing an interest in your private life implies showing interest in my guru's life. And that is natural and appropriate for me. Lady Chitralekha, you know well that your presence here threatens the calm, controlled peace of this hut. This establishment is like a family in which each of us has the right not only to criticise others' acts, but also to interfere in them."

"I am not bound by your code," Chitralekha said.

"True. Still, I will go to Beejgupta's place today—if nothing else, to meet my class-fellow, Shwetank. Lady, I beseech you again, do think about it. Take pity on us!"

"Pity?" Chitralekha snorted. "Do you even know who needs pity and from whom? You may as well ask for pity from the executioner, or creation from the destroyer. How wrong you are!" She choked and fled the spot.

When Vishaldeva returned from the city, Chitralekha was waiting for him. She lay listlessly under the banyan tree outside the hut. In spite of everything she had said on the matter, she still wanted to know about Beejgupta. She sat up as soon as she saw Vishaldeva approaching.

Vishaldeva went straight to her. "Lady Chitralekha," he said, "I did not meet Beejgupta, but I did talk to

Shwetank. I did not stop for long, because Shwetank was about to leave for Arya Mrityunjay's place. I walked with him, and we talked on the way, as he was in a hurry. When he got there, he went in, and I left."

"Did Shwetank also ask you about me?" Chitralekha asked.

"Oh yes. He asked many times about your health and well-being. He would even have come here if he was not in a hurry. And I can tell you one more thing: you will be surprised… He loves Yashodhara and wants to marry her!"

Chitralekha raised her eyebrows and stared at Vishaldeva. "Marry her? But Beejgupta has married her!"

Now Vishaldeva was surprised. "What made you think that? Shwetank clearly told me that Beejgupta was attracted to Yashodhara, but he will never marry her. His love for you is for ever."

Chitralekha took a deep breath and stood up. "Thank you, Vishaldeva. Please forgive the harsh words I have spoken to you. Believe me, I will leave today."

She strode into the hut. Vishaldeva muttered to himself, "She is a strange lady."

Kumargiri was lying, thinking about Chitralekha. He was not at ease. He saw Chitralekha enter, and sprang from his cot, trembling like a madman. "Where were you, my love? Come, come!"

Chitralekha's steely gaze cut through him. Her eyes were burning with distilled hatred and disgust. "Wretched animal! Stay away from me."

Kumargiri stepped back, stunned.

"You deceived me, you lustful insect! You lied to me. Your penances and meditation will come to nothing, and you will burn in hell! I am going. Don't try to stop me."

Kumargiri found his voice. "What I did, I did out of love for you. I was blinded."

"Did I not just call you a lustful insect? What do you know about love? You live for yourself; you are the centre of your existence. How can you know what love is? Love is sacrifice, giving up oneself and forgetting mine-ness. Your meditation and your austerity, your penance and your devotion—these are all false, miles away from the truth. You eschew the path of the householder, with its encumbrances, and it is cowardliness that drives you to create a pretence of being a sage. You think nothing of cheating me to sate your lust. Who are you to talk of love?"

Kumargiri could not bear this shower of insults. He stood erect. "Go, dancer! I do not need you. You made me fall, and now you make me rise as well. You defeated me—and I you. You lecture me, but look at yourself first! I know that you will not be able to sense the raw animal passion that glimmers in your face. Go, and take your cursed presence with you." He walked out of the hut, trembling with fury.

CHAPTER TWENTY-ONE

fter returning from Mrityunjay's palace, Shwetank reported his conversation with Vishaldeva to Beejgupta. Beejgupta did not reply.

"Should I not go and see the mistress?" Shwetank asked, when Beejgupta did not respond.

"No," Beejgupta was curt. "There is no point."

Shwetank sensed that Beejgupta was not interested talking about Chitralekha. He bowed and left.

Beejgupta's unease did not wane in Patliputra. It only increased. His heart was torn by two images. Chitralekha's flight had left an emptiness in his life. That emptiness was unbearable, and Yashodhara's appearance was a balm to his bruised soul. Now he wanted to accept Yashodhara—to marry her. But he had spurned her once. If he had to go back to Mrityunjay and ask for Yashodhara's hand, that would be a great defeat for him, and one that he could not bring himself to accept.

Beejgupta was a member of the Maurya empire's military council. After his return to Patliputra, he found himself listless and he could not concentrate on his official work. What started as a fleeting disturbance grew into a dull ache in his heart. He became a recluse and the crowds, the festivals, the delights of the city became repulsive to him.

He could not sleep that night. So Chitralekha was happy and hearty. And here he was, forlorn and sad. What a contrast. What a mistake. He may as well accept defeat. He must ask for Yashodhara. He must find an end to his loneliness.

For the first time, Shwetank had could put together the truth from Beejgupta's tone, his expression and his indifference to Chitralekha. Shwetank, too, was unable to sleep that night.

In the morning, Beejgupta rose from bed feeling light. He was a very happy man. He had set his mind on talking to Mrityunjay about Yashodhara. When he stepped out, he had his old smile on his face, and a stride in his step. When he sat down for breakfast, Shwetank was not there. He sent a servant to call him.

When Shwetank walked in, his face was pale. It was clear that he was miserable. "Shwetank, are you unwell?" Beejgupta asked.

"Sir I am well, but not happy," Shwetank said with his head bowed.

"What is the matter?" Beejgupta asked.

Shwetank pursed his lips and thought for a moment. Then he raised his head. "Master, you have been so kind to me. Only you can help me now."

Beejgupta chuckled. "Shwetank, you know that you are like a brother to me. I am ready to do what is within my powers for you."

"I know, sir, and that is why I have summoned the courage to ask you. Master! I want to marry Yashodhara."

Beejgupta was stunned, as if a thousand scorpions had stung him at the same time. For a few moments, his eyes turned glassy and he looked at Shwetank without saying a word. "What's that you say? You want to marry Yashodhara? And what help do you need from me?"

"Master, if you could take the proposal to Arya Mrityunjay?"

"You know, Shwetank, that Arya Mrityunjay put forward a proposal to me, and I refused it then because of Chitralekha. You also know that Chitralekha has now left me, and I am quite attracted to Yashodhara."

"I know, master! But I did not know that master's heart was open to marriage with Yashodhara."

"No—you cannot get what you ask for. I am in love with Yashodhara, and last night I decided to marry her." Beejgupta stared at Shwetank with his forehead lined and his eyebrows knit. His voice was loud and hoarse. "Do you even know what you are asking of me? Have I not gone through enough pain, enough heartbreak? Do you want me to ruin my life? No Shwetank! That is not possible. I will marry Yashodhara, and you had better get that through your head."

Shwetank's eyes watered. He joined his hands in prayer. "Master, I am guilty. Please forgive me. I exceeded my limits—please forgive me. You are big-hearted; please forgive me."

"Don't drive me mad, Shwetank!" Beejgupta shouted. "Go away. I request you, just go!"

Shwetank walked away slowly.

Beejgupta smacked his head. "Oh, my stars." He whispered to himself, "No, no, Shwetank! This cannot be. I shall marry. I shall marry. Don't I have the right to happiness?"

He stood up. "I will go now," he said. "No one can stop me. I have decided to marry Yashodhara—now there is no going back." Beejgupta called for his chariot.

Then he started thinking. What right did Shwetank have to love Yashodhara? Did he not know that his master was drawn to her? Beejgupta's body burned and his throat was parched. He gulped down a glass of cool water and became less agitated. He slowed his breath and focused his mind. What was Shwetank's crime? It was natural for him to love. He was a young man, a human of flesh and blood, and natural instincts. And how could he know that Beejgupta's love for Chitralekha was strangled?

But was it? His thought swerved. "Am I so weak and fickle that I loved one woman and now I love another? Is love really ephemeral?"

Beejgupta was confused now. He did not want to admit that love is not immortal, even though by now he had experienced its mortal nature. "No," he said to himself, "love is permanent. Then what drives me to do what I am doing? Is it to get even with Chitralekha? No, I do not carry any grudge against her."

The chariot was ready. Beejgupta boarded it and moved towards Mrityunjay's mansion. His mind worked feverishly. Was this what self-control meant? Each man for himself—was this how the world worked? If so, how were men different from animals? If every creature lived for itself, how was he different from other creatures? What would be the outcome of his marriage to Yashodhara? One young man would be shattered, his life ruined. And this man, Shwetank was like a brother. Beejgupta would fall from his own ideals. Would he be able to love Yashodhara? He was troubled now, and he wanted to marry Yashodhara to put his sorrows behind him. But what of the future? No, he had no right to marry her, he realised. He had no right to cast a shadow on Shwetank's life. Beejgupta had decided his path, after thinking it through. Now he must tread the path, irrespective of whether he found success or failure, joy or misery. He would be a coward—no, a villain—if he pushed Shwetank into unhappiness just to have a chance of happiness for himself. He was being unjust to others and to himself. Good and bad were part of his fate. He must face them with equanimity.

The chariot jolted to a halt and he saw that he was at Mrityunjay's mansion. He sent word that he was at the gate. Mrityunjay came out to welcome him and accompany him inside. After they had settled down, Mrityunjay asked, "What made Arya Beejgupta bless my home with his presence today?"

Beejgupta chose his words carefully. "Arya Mrityunjay, I have come to you with a proposal for your daughter's wedding."

Mrityunjay's face was creased with a broad smile. "Arya Beejgupta, I am all ears."

Beejgupta knew what Mrityunjay was thinking. "Arya Mrityunjay, I am not here to talk about myself. I bring the proposal that you give your daughter in marriage to Shwetank. Shwetank is from a high family. He is handsome, well-behaved and educated. He will be a suitable match for your daughter—perhaps more than me."

Mrityunjay's usually stoic face betrayed his surprise. Many moments passed before he spoke in a controlled and polite manner. "Arya Beejgupta, Shwetank is capable, but he is not from a wealthy family. He has no assets that I know of. I cannot even consider your proposal."

Beejgupta was surprised now. "But Arya Mrityunjay," he said, "you yourself are fortunate to have great wealth, and you do not have any heir except Yashodhara."

Mrityunjay smiled. "No, Arya Beejgupta. Yashodhara has no claim on my property. I have an adopted son, whom you have not met as he is away on a campaign. He will be my inheritor. Why don't you marry Yashodhara yourself? I have seen that she likes you."

"No, I shall not marry, Arya Mrityunjay. Is Yashodhara's marriage to Shwetank impossible?"

Mrityunjay sighed. "Yes, Arya Beejgupta. I do consider him suitable, but I cannot marry Yashodhara to him as he is too poor. It will not be fair to her."

Beejgupta pondered over this. Then he said, "Arya Mrityunjay, I will adopt Shwetank. That way he will get a claim on my property. I trust that changes the situation and you have no objection to Shwetank as a son-in-law?"

"But no, Arya Beejgupta, that is not possible. You are still very young! It is completely possible that you will marry later, and your son will then displace Shwetank as your heir."

"You are right, sir. Though I am bent against getting married at this point in time, who knows my state of mind later? But I do want Shwetank and Yashodhara to be married, and I can ready to do whatever it takes to make that possible. Arya Mrityunjay, I will give all my property to Shwetank."

Mrityunjay was stunned. He gestured with his hands and gulped before he said, "You do not know what you are saying, Arya Beejgupta! You are not well."

"Don't worry about me, sir," Beejgupta said. "I have said in your presence that I will transfer all my property to Shwetank. You yourself are the witness. As for my title, transferring it will require the emperor's permission. I will get it today. Now you should not have any objection to the proposal."

Mrityunjay leaned forward and looked at Beejgupta with wide, troubled eyes. "Think for a moment, Beejgupta! Once I accept your proposal, I will hold you to it. You will not be able to back out of it."

Beejgupta held his gaze and spoke in a firm tone, each word soft but emphatic. "Arya Mrityunjay, I will keep my word. I do not know what it is to go back on a promise."

"Then I accept your proposal," Mrityunjay said in a trembling voice.

Beejgupta stood up. "I shall take your leave then. The letter of donation and the decree for the title will be ready today. There is no need to delay things. Please decide the date of the marriage."

Mrityunjay stood up shakily. "Arya Beejgupta," he said, "I am a man of the world. Believe me when I say this: you are a god, not a man." His eyes were moist.

Beejgupta saluted him with a *namaste* and left. When he reached home, he went to Shwetank's room. Shwetank was asleep. The sheet over his head was damp with tears. Beejgupta shook him awake, and he woke up with a start.

"Master, what is your command?" he asked.

"Do not address me as Master, Courtier Shwetank!"

"What do you mean, sir?" Shwetank gulped, and asked, half-asleep.

"I mean what I say. Listen! I took a proposal for you to marry Yashodhara to Arya Mrityunjay. He had some objections to the idea. To address his objections, I have donated my property and title to you. He has agreed to the proposal."

For some time, Shwetank stood still and lifeless, looking at Beejgupta. Then he broke into tears. "No, no! Master, I do not accept this. Oh, what a sinner I am—master, please forgive me. I will ruin your life this way. Why must you be so generous to a lowly man like me? I do not accept this at all!" He fell at Beejgupta's feet.

Beejgupta picked him up and patted his shoulder. "Shwetank, what had to happen has happened. Now, if you have the slightest affection for me, just accept what I am doing. Do not make a me charlatan in the eyes of the world. I have enjoyed this glamour enough. Now my mind is satiated. I request you, do not turn down my gift. Come, you must accompany me to the palace and complete the formalities."

CHAPTER TWENTY-TWO

hitralekha returned to the city, but she could not bring herself to meet Beejgupta. She did not have the courage. She felt she had wronged him. She went straight to her place.

She now led a spiritual life in the house which had once been a centre for sensuousness. She sought solace in her new life, and she was happy to bask in the fire of repentance. Gradually, she sank into depression, and she found herself spending her days and nights weeping.

She loved Beejgupta. She realised how deep her love was after the days of separation. But she had tainted herself by giving in to Kumargiri in his moment of madness and stupidity. She loved Beejgupta so much that she could not deceive him for an instant. She had betrayed him, and she felt the just reward for this sin was the agony that she was living through. The more she was scorched by the flames of her penitence, the more succour she found. The more she cried, the more she felt at peace.

A month passed. One day, as she sat crying, a maid informed her that Shwetank wanted to see her.

She stood up, startled. Had Beejgupta called her? "Where is he? I am coming!" she said.

Shwetank waited for Chitralekha in the guest room. He hid his surprise when he saw her. She had become a shadow of her glamorous form. If he had not been expecting her, he may not have recognised her. "Lady, you do not look well at all," he said. "Why are you in this condition?"

"I am fine," Chitralekha said, and sat down.

They were both lost for words. Chitralekha broke the silence. "Is Arya Beejgupta well?"

Shwetank frowned. "Yes, he is well. But he has changed a lot."

"Changed?" Chitralekha was worried. "How has he changed? Has he married?"

"No, he has not married," Shwetank said with a wry smile. "I am the one who is getting married. I will marry courtier Mrityunjay's daughter Yashodhara, and I came to invite you to the wedding. But Arya Beejgupta has made a divine sacrifice. Courtier Mrityunjay did not want this marriage at first, because I was poor. Arya Beejgupta has donated his title and all his wealth to me. He is about to leave Patliputra. He will only stay till the wedding.

Chitralekha heart thudded, and her eyes filled with tears. "Did Beejgupta do so much? You do know, Shwetank, that it is a great sacrifice? And I am the cause of it... Anyway, I congratulate you. When is the wedding?"

"It will be completed next week, on Sunday. There is a feast on Tuesday. The emperor, courtiers and officials will come. Lady, your presence is essential."

Chitralekha said, "Shwetank, you must excuse me. I will come some other day, but not for the feast. I have taken to a different life—that celebration is not for me."

"But lady Chitralekha, you have called me a brother! And this is a request."

"I cannot grant your request, Shwetank. You know that my resolve does not waver. I have a sister's affection for you—that of an elder sister. I shall come some other day."

"As you wish. But you should know that Arya Beejgupta will leave the city that night, to become a wanderer. Do think about it."

"Arya Beejgupta will leave that night..." Chitralekha eyes grew moist again. But then she took a deep breath. "That does not change my decision," she said.

The wedding was as grand as it was expected to be. The emperor and other dignitaries attended the celebration. Beejgupta played the role of host to perfection that evening. He laughed often, but his heart was heavy. Chitralekha's absence hurt him. He wanted to see her before leaving Patliputra for ever, but she did not come.

After the feast, the emperor congratulated Shwetank, and addressed him as a courtier. Then he sought out Beejgupta and summoned him. He took

Beejgupta's hands in his, and stood up. The whole assembly rose along with him. The hubbub of the party halted, replaced by a pin-drop silence. The emperor said, "Beejgupta, you are a great soul. You have shown us that the impossible can be made possible. You have become a god. Today, the ruler of India, this emperor Chandragupta Maurya, bows his head before you." The emperor bowed reverentially before Beejgupta. All the guests followed the emperors example. From among the women, a few muffled sobs broke out. The atmosphere was charged.

Beejgupta bowed to the emperor and said, "King of kings, I do not deserve this honour. I leave tonight to wander the country as a beggar, and your blessings are all I need."

With that, Beejgupta walked towards the main door. The guests lined up on both sides with their palms joined in respect. Beejgupta glowed like a man who was completely at peace. Beejgupta crossed the threshold that defined the boundary of power and splendour with grace.

Beejgupta's servants stood outside. They wept when they saw him. He stopped and looked at each of them, and said to them, "Treat Shwetank as you have treated me. And try to forget me."

The servants cried even louder. A few of them said, "We will come with you!"

"What's that?" Beejgupta said gravely. "Not a single one of you will leave with me. You have orders to stay."

They shrank back, and Beejgupta walked on. It was past midnight. Beejgupta went on foot, like a beggar. He

walked slowly. The city was quiet. Beejgupta wore ordinary clothes, and he had a few silver coins with him. He
heard footsteps behind him, and soon they came closer.
Beejgupta looked over his shoulder, but could not see
anyone. He kept walking.

The footsteps were very close now. Beejgupta
turned to see a figure cloaked in plain cloth. "My lord!"
the figure called out in a dry voice.

Beejgupta stood still. "Who is it?" he called out.

"My lord! My lord! Forgive me!" The figure fell at
Beejgupta's feet.

"Chitralekha!" Beejgupta said in a harsh voice.
"The curse of my life! What brings you here? Go away.
It's too late now. What brought you here?"

"I want to kiss your feet!" I want to worship you!"
Chitralekha said in a broken voice. "My lord, I have ruined your life, I have reduced you to a beggar. Curse me,
punish me, hit me—but don't hate me."

Beejgupta's whole body trembled. He said with a
choked throat, "Chitralekha, it is over. You finished it
for good. You did not come back to me after leaving Kumargiri's hut. I lost all hope. Now, you come to sway me
from my wandering—why? I have nothing to give you
now, neither ardour nor means. Let me go!"

Chitralekha gripped his hand. "No, I will not let
you go, master. You must stay one day as my guest. If
you have to go, go tomorrow."

Beejgupta wrenched his hand away. "Get away
from me, dancer! You cannot stop me now. Look at your
destructive powers! Laugh at me! Go, and let me leave."
Beejgupta started walking.

Chitralekha held on to his feet. "I will not let you go. You must come with me to my house. Beejgupta, my love, have you completely extinguished your love for me? Tell me, my lord..." Chitralekha broke down and her body convulsed as she sobbed bitterly.

Beejgupta slumped and reached for her shoulder. "If my love was dead, why would I leave my old world behind? Chitralekha, I wanted to stamp out my love for you, but I couldn't! I can't!" He helped her up and moved to embrace her, but she stepped back.

"No, master!" Chitralekha said. "Do not touch me. I am impure, tainted, a sinner, my lord. Come, come to my house and purify me. Scorch me in the fire of your curse!"

Beejgupta spoke involuntarily. "Come, let us go," he said. "You are the one person in this world whom I cannot say no to. Pull me down as much as you like—but give me your word that you will not stop me tomorrow."

"I promise," Chitralekha said.

When they reached Chitralekha's house, she made arrangements for him to sleep. "Master, go to sleep now. I have much to talk about, but I will talk in the morning." Beejgupta looked at her, speechless, as she turned and left.

Early in the morning, Chitralekha came to him. "Master, I have come to sit at your feet."

Beejgupta was perplexed by her behaviour. "Why? Why have you changed so much?" he asked.

"I have to sanctify myself," Chitralekha said. "My master, I have already strayed from my true path. I became the means to satisfy yogi Kumargiri's lust. I surrendered my body to him in a fit of rage. I need to cleanse this body of mine." Chitralekha told Beejgupta her story. "Now you know, lord, why I did not come to you. Please forgive me."

"Is that all?" Beejgupta said with a laugh. "Chitralekha, you have erred greatly. You have misunderstood me. You ask for my forgiveness? Chitralekha! Love is sacrifice, oblivion, union. In the court of love there is no crime. Forgive you for what? In any case, if you want forgiveness, here you are: I forgive you."

Chitralekha gripped Beejgupta's feet. "Master, then accept me!" she said.

"How can I do that, lady Chitralekha?" Beejgupta asked. "I am now a beggar and an ascetic. How can I do that now?"

"But I have immense wealth! I am yours. My property will be yours. Why do you think you are poor? Why do you call yourself a beggar?"

"Your property? Your wealth? These are no use to me. I have left the world of the senses, not to submerge myself in it again, but to abandon it for ever. I can only accept you as a beggar."

Chitralekha stood up. "Let it be so, then. Let us wander as beggars. I will give away everything I have today. Tonight, we will start our voyage on the endless sea of the world in our love boat." Chitralekha's face glowed, and her eyes shone with the brilliance of one who has attained enlightenment.

Beejgupta kissed her. "How happy we are!"

Epilogue

ne year later...

The great Ratnambar spoke. "Young man Shwetank, you are married, and now you have a family. Can you tell me which man, Beejgupta or Kumargiri, is a sinner?"

Shwetank bowed his head. "Great guru," he said, "Beejgupta is a god-like man. He is the epitome of sacrifice. He has a large heart. But Kumargiri—he is an animal. He lives for himself. The world gains no benefit from his life. He goes against the laws of nature. He shirks the challenges of the world to find peace for himself. Kumargiri is a sinner!"

"And Vishaldeva?" Ratnambar said. "You took initiation under Kumargiri and became a yogi. Now let's hear your answer—between Kumargiri and Beejgupta, who is the sinner?"

Vishaldeva bowed to Ratnambar, and said, "Great guru, Yogi Kumargiri is invincible. He has triumphed over mine-ness. He has risen above the realm of the senses. His spirituality, his knowledge, his energy—these virtues are complete and whole. Meanwhile, Beejgupta has lived the life of a slave of desire, a life devoted to the hateful world of sensuousness. He is a sinner, a pillar of the sinful world!"

Ratnambar spoke with equanimity. "You both lived in different circumstances, and your concepts of sin differ. Now that you are about to depart, your education is complete. Before you go, listen to my last lesson.

"There is nothing sinful in the world. Sin is another name for a different point of view. Each of us is born with a specific, innate inclination of the mind. Each one comes to enact his or her role on the world's stage. We follow the script that is inspired by the working of our mind—that is our life. So, we do according to our inclination, and inclination is shaped by our nature. We are not our own masters; we are slaves of circumstances. We are bound by circumstances. We are not doers; we are instruments. So what of sin and virtue?

"We are ruled by attachment to ourselves. We want happiness. In that, we are all the same. Only the centres of happiness differ. Some see happiness in wealth; some see it in wine. Some seek happiness in what others call loose conduct; some seek it in sacrifice. But we all seek happiness. We do not voluntarily act to inflict sorrow on ourselves. This is human nature, and this is where viewpoints diverge.

"In this world, there is no definition of sin—and there never will be. We do not sin, and we do not perform virtuous deeds. We only do what we must do."

Ratnambar stood up. "This is my view. You may or may not agree with it. I do not compel you to agree, nor is it within my powers. Go, and be happy!"

Afterword

Disentangling Sin and Virtue

ho knows—from a moral viewpoint—what is right and what is wrong? Today it is easy to say, and to accept, that we should not be quick to judge; that the circumstances determine whether a choice is right.

When Chitralekha[1] was published, in 1934, it was probably not as easy to take this nuanced stance. The story of the tangled lives of Chitralekha, Beejgupta and Kumargiri revolves around this question: What is sin? Bhagwati Charan Verma (1903-1981) opens the story with a thesis, veers to the anti-thesis and finally ends with a synthesis, when Ratnambar reveals his thoughts on the nature of sin.

The 1930s was a period when India was going through a second era of transformation in its modern history. The dynamics that were forging its society

---

1 Chitralekha is the title of the Hindi novel that this book is a translation of. For this translation, we have used a title that is more meaningful to readers who have not yet read the text.

included the independence struggle, social progress, displacement, urbanisation, political and cultural divides and advances in transportation and publishing. In the course of the movement towards progress and modernity, society faced off with antagonistic foreign social, political and economic forces; but the conflict with entrenched, indigenous cultures and beliefs was no less intense. In the Indian subconscious, sin and virtue—and hence right and wrong—are strangely tied to carnal attraction and the purity of the body. Modernity has not brought freedom from tradition in its wake. Even today, the modern Indian world-view is tinted by tradition.

In the social and cultural ferment of 1934, there were doubts about the conventional, reassuring answers to the central question of sin versus virtue, but the question itself had not been squarely addressed in the literature.

The published fiction in Hindi had evolved from its origins in the magical-adventure-fantasy genre to Premchand's themes of idealism expressed against a backdrop of social realism. Jaishankar Prasad's plays drew on historical characters to cloak powerful messages calling for political awakening and aspirations for independence. *Chitralekha* burst on to this literary scene with a completely new paradigm.

It was a time of change. A whole generation of students had gone through a formal education in English by the 1930s. English and world literature had influenced them, but their daily lives were still led on foundations of a unified and simplistic body of thought that tied together man-woman relationships, celibacy, meditation, purity and sacredness—a not unexpected outcome of belief in eternal certitudes. Even if the concerns and complexities that challenged overly simple beliefs had seeped into everyday life, they were not yet acknowledged or addressed in the world of letters.

Chitralekha took these concerns and framed them in the form of the question of sin versus virtue, using the distant Mauryan period as a canvas. With *Chitralekha*, Verma had set a precedent that other contemporary writers would follow. Jaishankar Prasad's *Dhruvswamini*, for example, also raised questions on virtuous love and purity of the body, and drew inspiration and acceptance from the ancient past and from Hindu scriptures.

There is another interesting aspect to *Chitralekha*. When Bhagwati Charan Verma was a student at Allahabad University, his friend and room-mate Bhagwan Sahay read Anatole France's *Thais*. He was so overcome by France's novel that he said Indian writers had very limited possibilities because the Western writers hadn't left much for them to enquire about.

In response to his friend's assertion, Bhagwati Charan Verma read *Thais*. He commented that perhaps Indian writers had not been left much to enquire about, but soon they would.

These events led to speculation, which culminated in a myth about the relationship between the *Thais* and *Chitralekha*. Perhaps the instant fame of *Chitralekha*, and its tumultuous reception, created a backlash of envy and some critics placed *Chitralekha* under the shadow of *Thais*. However, the essential issues of literary creation include story arch, setting, character and voice. On each of these aspects, the two literary works differ. When he talked about the idea of *Chitralekha*, Bhagwati Charan Verma himself gave credit to his conversations with Bhagwan Sahay out of gratitude—and perhaps to protect himself from future charges of being overly influenced by *Thais*. It is true that *Thais* helped him train his creative powers on sin and virtue in the realm of the senses. Thais is an actress and a courtesan; Chitralekha is a court dancer. An ascetic enters their lives and is tested. The primary questions of both works are similar. In times of transition, cultural exchanges and external influences are quite natural.

The differences between the two works start with their story arches. Anatole France's Paphnutius is an ascetic who takes pride in his virtue and purity. He wants to convert and uplift Thais, and he sets out from his desert land to seek her in Alexandria. He had known her much earlier. Thais has become an actress and a prostitute, and she lives a debauched life.

Paphnutius sees her in the guise of a handsome, well-groomed youth and engages her in discussions on the spiritual and the eternal. Surprisingly, he is able to convert her to Christianity.

Thais turns out to be more contemplative than him. She adopts the ascetic life and enters a convent. She completes her atonement for the past after three years of solitary penance. She is accepted by the nuns, but she has a spiritual experience so intense that it kills her only fourteen days after being ordained.

In the meantime, Paphnutius himself is enthralled by her aura, and is unable to free himself from his infatuation. He strays from his values. On the verge of her death, when Thais sees the gates of heaven open for her, Paphnutius tells her that his faith is a pretence, and that he loves her.

Interestingly, of the two philosophers and thinkers that the protagonist meets, Timocles is depicted as meditating while sitting in the *padmaasan* posture adopted by Hindu sages. He has not heard of Christ, and he is pictured as a skeptic. His views echo the Jain pluralist *syaadvaad* stream of thought, in which everything is considered multi-faceted and nothing can be definitively known. As stated earlier, in times of change, cultural exchanges and external influences are common—and they can flow in multiple directions.

As the noted Hindi writer Shrilal Shukla has observed[2], *Chitralekha* is more dramatic than *Thais*, and more entertaining to the average reader. Eschewing a heavy analysis of sin and virtue, *Chitralekha* draws on the traditional folk tale format in which two or three princes set out on difficult journeys, in completely different directions, to seek something rare. Bhagwati Charan Verma's skilful use of this device, larger-than-life characters, clear descriptions and sensitive use of language made Chitralekha a landmark Hindi novel, one that was "crisp and enthralling in spite of a serious theme."

---

2   Shrilal Shukla (1994), Bhagwati Charan Verma (Tripti Jain, Trans.). Sahitya Akademi: Delhi, India.

When he wrote *Chitralekha*, Bhagwati Charan Verma was practicing law in Hamirpur, a small town near Kanpur (a town much better known to Indians). He had some published works to his credit, but Chitralekha gave him unparalleled acclaim. He became a full-time writer after this success. Bhagwati Charan Verma worked for Bombay Talkies, a movie studio founded in 1934, and wrote scripts for several films including *Kismet* (1943), *Hamaari Baat* (1943), *Jwaar Bhaataa* (1944) and *Pratima* (1945). Two Hindi films were based on *Chitralekha*. In 1950, he returned to Lucknow (the capital of Uttar Pradesh state) and devoted himself to literature. He produced more than fifty works of prose, fiction and autobiography. He won many awards and honours, and was nominated to be a member of the Rajya Sabha, the upper house of the Indian parliament.

These are great achievements, but *Chitralekha* towers over them all.

Dr. Archana Verma
Ghaziabad, India
10 June 2015
Email: mamushu46@gmail.com

GLOSSARY

Apsara	Nymph
Arya	Noble person
Brahma	The creator god in the Hindu trilogy of Brahma, Vishnu and Shiva; also the state of pure awareness
Brahman	Priestly caste
Chitralekha	One a beautiful as a picture
Gandharva	Male nature spirits
Kshatriya	Warrior caste
Loo	Hot, dry summer wind
Maya	The physical, illusory world
Mridang	Percussion instrument played with hands, from the sides
Namaste	Traditional Indian greeting, made by bringing the palms together before the chest and bowing

Raaga   Series of notes with which a musical melody
                is constructed in Indian classical music.

Saarangi   Stringed instrument played with a bow

Shahnai   Wind instrument similar to the oboe

Shudra   "Lower" caste, that served the other castes

Veena   Plucked string instrument

Tabla   Percussion instrument played with hands,
                from the top

Yagya   Prayer ceremony; religious ritual performed
                in front of a sacred fire

Printed in the USA
CPSIA information can be obtained
at www.ICGtesting.com
LVHW061032170823
755520LV00016B/188

9 789810 994426